Theoretical Dragon Anatomy

Structure & Function

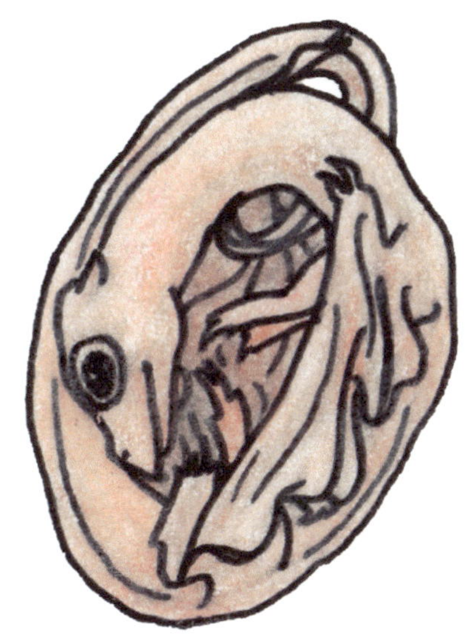

Isabelle V. Busch

Copyright © 2019 Isabelle V. Busch

All rights reserved. No part of this publication may be reproduced or transmitted in any form or by any means, electronic or mechanical, including information storage and retrieval and photographic or recording systems, without permission in writing from the publisher (except by reviewers, who may quote brief passages in a review). Researchers and teachers may also utilize elements for educational purposes.

ISBN 978-0-9986610-9-4 (Hardback Edition)

Cover design by Isabelle V. Busch
All illustrations, graphics and text by Isabelle V. Busch
Author photograph © Chris Thompson

Printed and bound in the United States of America
First printing June 2019

Published by Episode Media
Spokane, WA

Visit www.isabellebusch.com for more information.

Theoretical Dragon Anatomy

Structure & Function

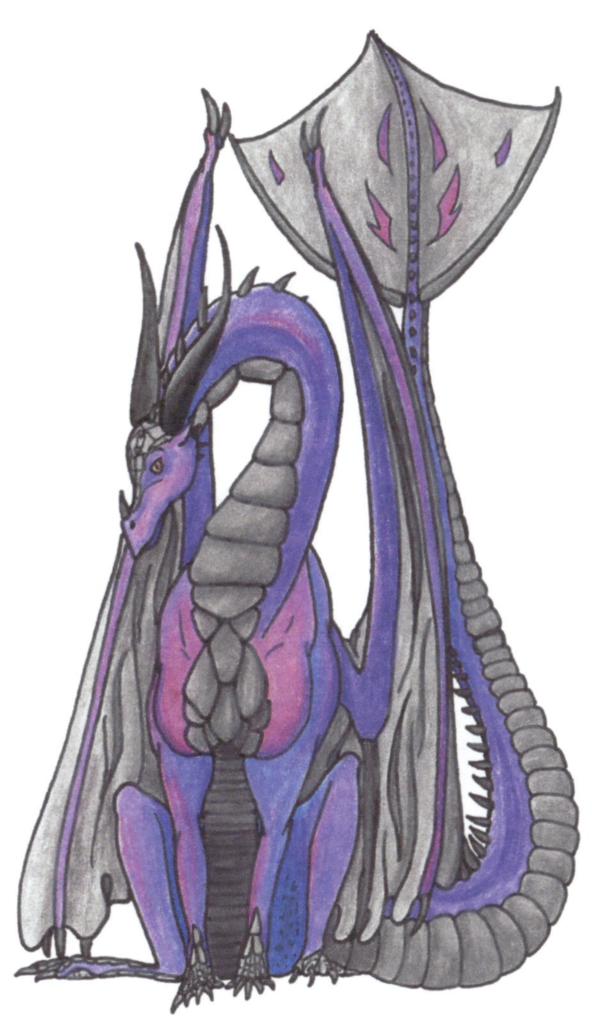

– written and illustrated by Isabelle V. Busch –

to those who relish and savor
unbounded curiosity

Acknowledgments

This book was three long years of work. Through all that time, I had support and encouragement. For this, above all, I would like to thank my parents from the bottom of my heart. You read and edited countless times, always catching what I missed. I love you Mom and Dad! Thanks also go out to my brother and peers at school for providing me with so many of the ideas for my pages. Your curiosity kept me going. I am grateful for the support of the staff at my school that believed in my book as well. Mr. Cantlon, thank you for pushing me to write this book. Carolyn, you were my best editor, providing me with improvements *and* cookies! Mr. Bock, thank you for always saving the day when it came to graphics. John Waite, your advice on all things books was invaluable for my book's success. The local author community was also an invaluable resource when it came to the publishing process. Finally, thanks to you. Reading is what this book was written for!

Preface

The writing of this book was prompted by curiosities sparked long ago. I have always found science fascinating, but anatomy opened up a whole new door for me in seventh grade, thanks to my teacher Mike Cantlon. When he presented our class with an independent project in eighth grade, I snagged my chance to pursue my interest in anatomy. Since we were allowed to do our project on literally anything–from goby fish to racquetball to the history of marshmallows–I decided to do mine on theoretical dragon anatomy. I blazed a new trail, drawing up my own diagrams with insights from extensive real world research, not other dragon diagrams. Mr. Cantlon loved my project, and insisted I make it into a book. So in tenth grade, I set aside a class just for that. This book is the product of that class: research, ponderings, drawings and an endless search for anatomical knowledge. I hope that it inspires you just as Mr. Cantlon inspired me.

Table of Contents

Introduction

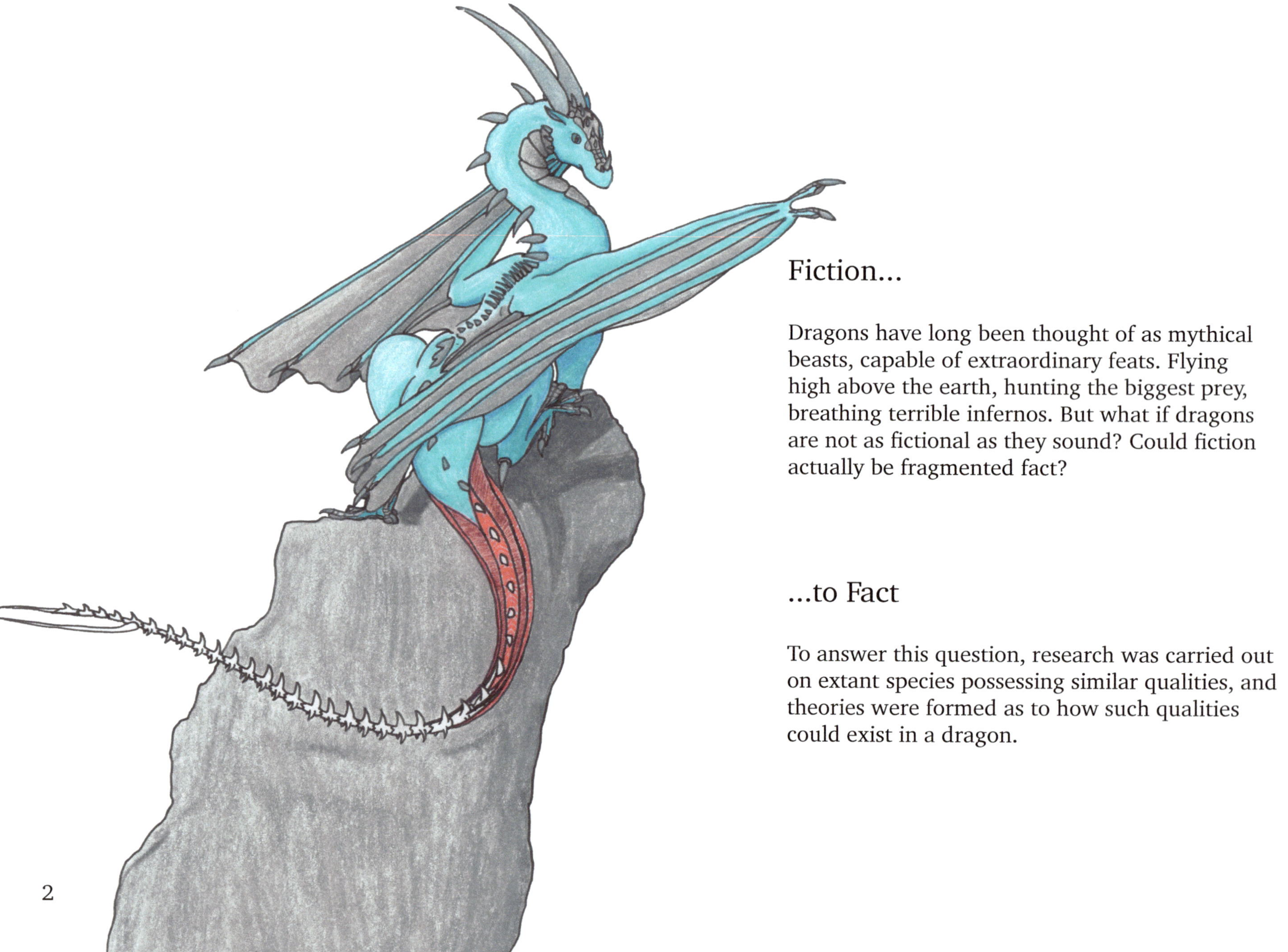

Fiction...

Dragons have long been thought of as mythical beasts, capable of extraordinary feats. Flying high above the earth, hunting the biggest prey, breathing terrible infernos. But what if dragons are not as fictional as they sound? Could fiction actually be fragmented fact?

...to Fact

To answer this question, research was carried out on extant species possessing similar qualities, and theories were formed as to how such qualities could exist in a dragon.

Organization

The material in this book examines certain adaptations and
anatomical features that dragons would possess, and explains
how they benefit the creatures. Each section starts with a full-
body diagram of an essential body system or group of systems.
There are four sections: skin, muscles, skeleton and organs. Full-
body diagrams are followed by examinations of specific body
structures.

Ready?

Throughout this book, examine dragons' most interesting
features, deadliest instincts, and most intelligent behaviors.
Learn what makes a dragon a dragon, how it does what it does,
and why. Dragons may be more real than you think.

A Closer Look at...

The Life Cycle

Dragons have a complex life cycle that ensures the survival of only the fittest individuals.

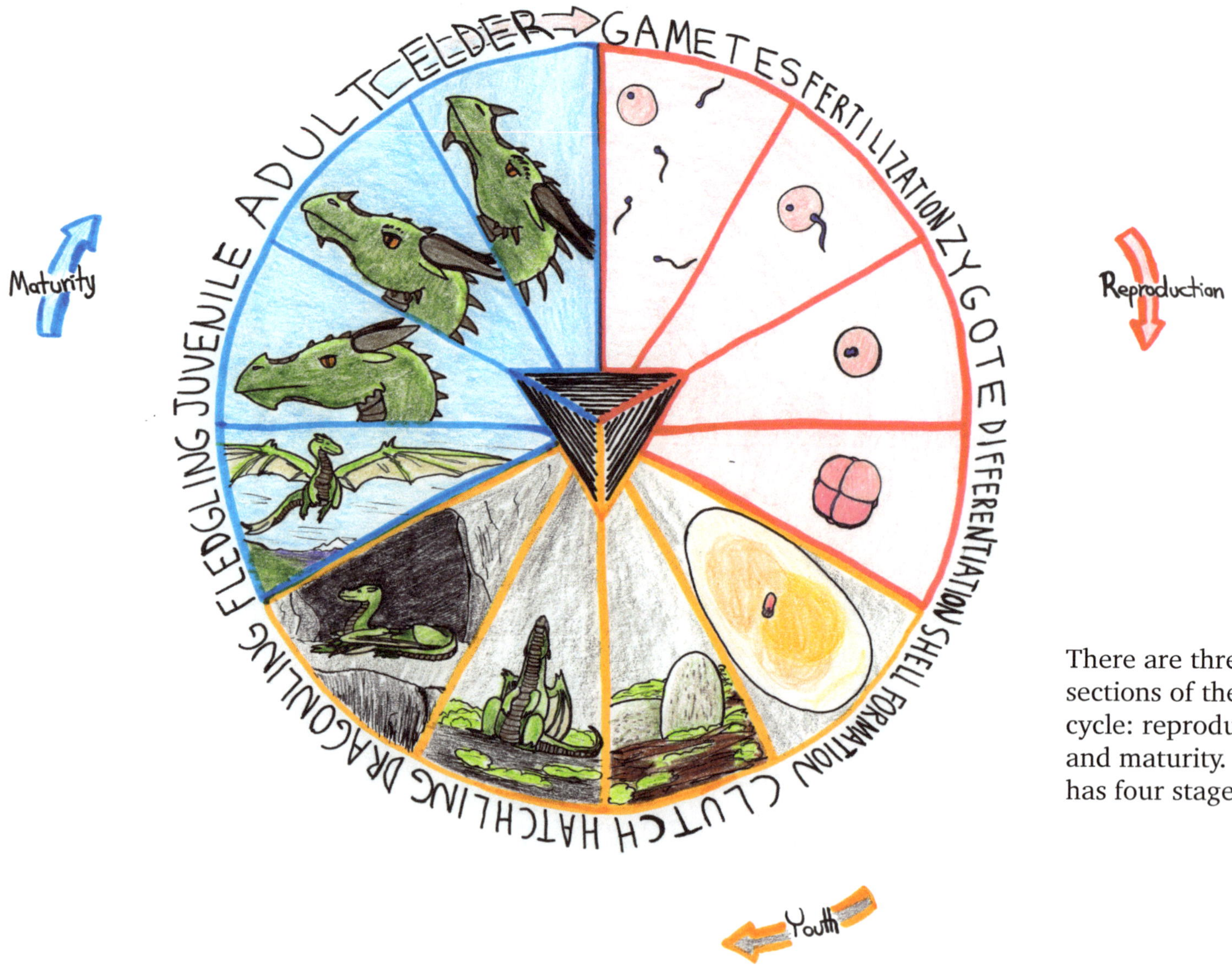

There are three main sections of the dragon life cycle: reproduction, youth and maturity. Each section has four stages.

The Twelve Stages

To better understand a dragon's life cycle, let's examine it from start to finish. The cycle starts with two adults successfully breeding and producing offspring.

1) The male and female produce gametes (egg and sperm) individually.

2) During mating, the male's sperm fertilizes the female's eggs. Each egg is now a zygote (union of egg and sperm).

3) The zygote develops into an embryo through cleavage, divisions that form new cells.

4) Through differentiation, the embryo establishes a distinct head-tail axis and begins forming specific anatomical structures, such as legs, wings, eyes and a heart.

5) At this stage of development, membranes and a mineral shell are deposited around the embryo.

6) The egg is laid through the tail's cloaca. Now in the nest, the egg continues to develop.

7) Once too big for the egg, the dragon hatches with the aid of its egg tooth. This freshly hatched, helpless dragon is aptly known as a hatchling.

8) After several weeks, the hatchling is slightly more independent, and is known as a dragonling.

9) Once the dragonling's wings have grown enough to support its body weight, it is able to fly, and is known as a fledgling.

10) Once the fledgling has learned enough skills from its parents to become fully independent, it leaves the nest to live on its own. At this stage of its life, it is known as a juvenile.

11) After about seven years on its own, the juvenile becomes sexually mature, and is officially an adult, able to breed with other adults.

12) Adults, after experiencing up to a century of adulthood, are no longer able to reproduce. At this point, the dragon is an elder. Many elders maintain a healthy, successful population by mentoring young or injured dragons.

The Skin:

An Inside Look

Skin Saves the Day

Skin has many purposes, although it at first seems to simply cover muscles and bone. In fact, the skin makes up the first line of defense in the immune system. The skin keeps unwanted particles and pathogens out of the body, keeping a dragon's health at its best. Understandably, a cut in the skin is a breach in the dragon's defenses, and is quickly sealed and repaired by blood clots, or scabs. Skin also protects the body from bigger threats. A rival dragon can pose just as large a risk of injury as a virus, so dragon skin is extremely rough, thick and tough, similar to that of a rhinoceros, elephant, or crocodile. But its durability is not owed only to its thickness. Dragon skin also sports many scutes, growths that drastically increase protection. Scutes blanket a dragon's most vulnerable regions. They cover the belly, undersides of the neck and tail, and both the tops and bottoms of the head, feet, and toes. Specialized scutes with bony bases are classified as osteoderms. Together, these growths serve as armor, thwarting rival dragons' attacks or other sources of injury.

Impressive ISOs

The skin also contains an intricate network of sensory organs. Nerves run throughout the skin, just as in humans, and channel sensory information to the brain. However, scutes are too thick to be felt through. So, scutes have a hole that the touch information can pass through. A small pore is present in each osteoderm or scute, often with a hair growing out of it, that detects movement and passes the information to a nerve. These sensory pores are called integumentary sensor organs, or ISOs. Providing a detailed sensory picture of the environment, ISOs are present in avid swimmers such as alligators and crocodiles, and serve the same function in dragons.

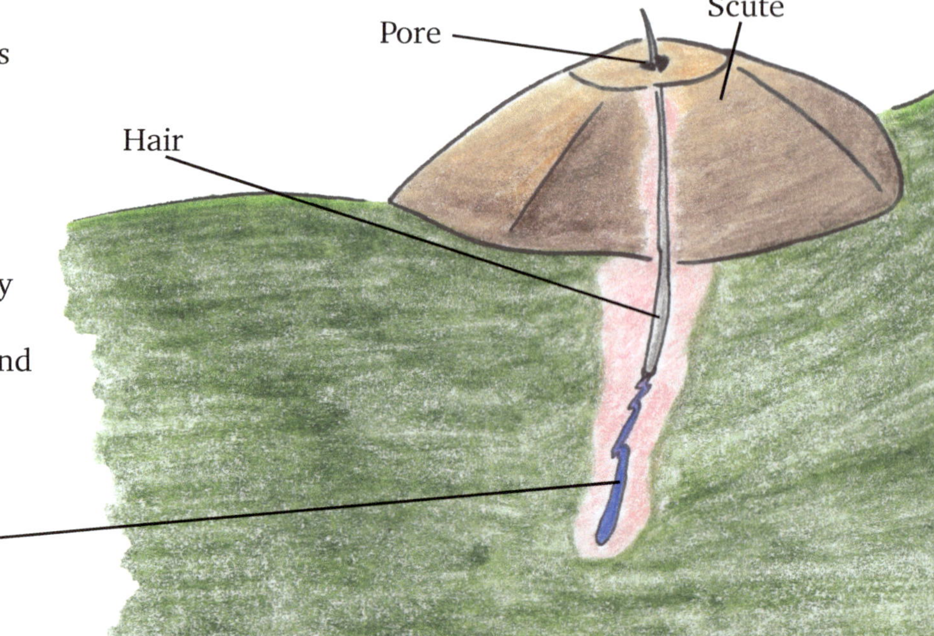

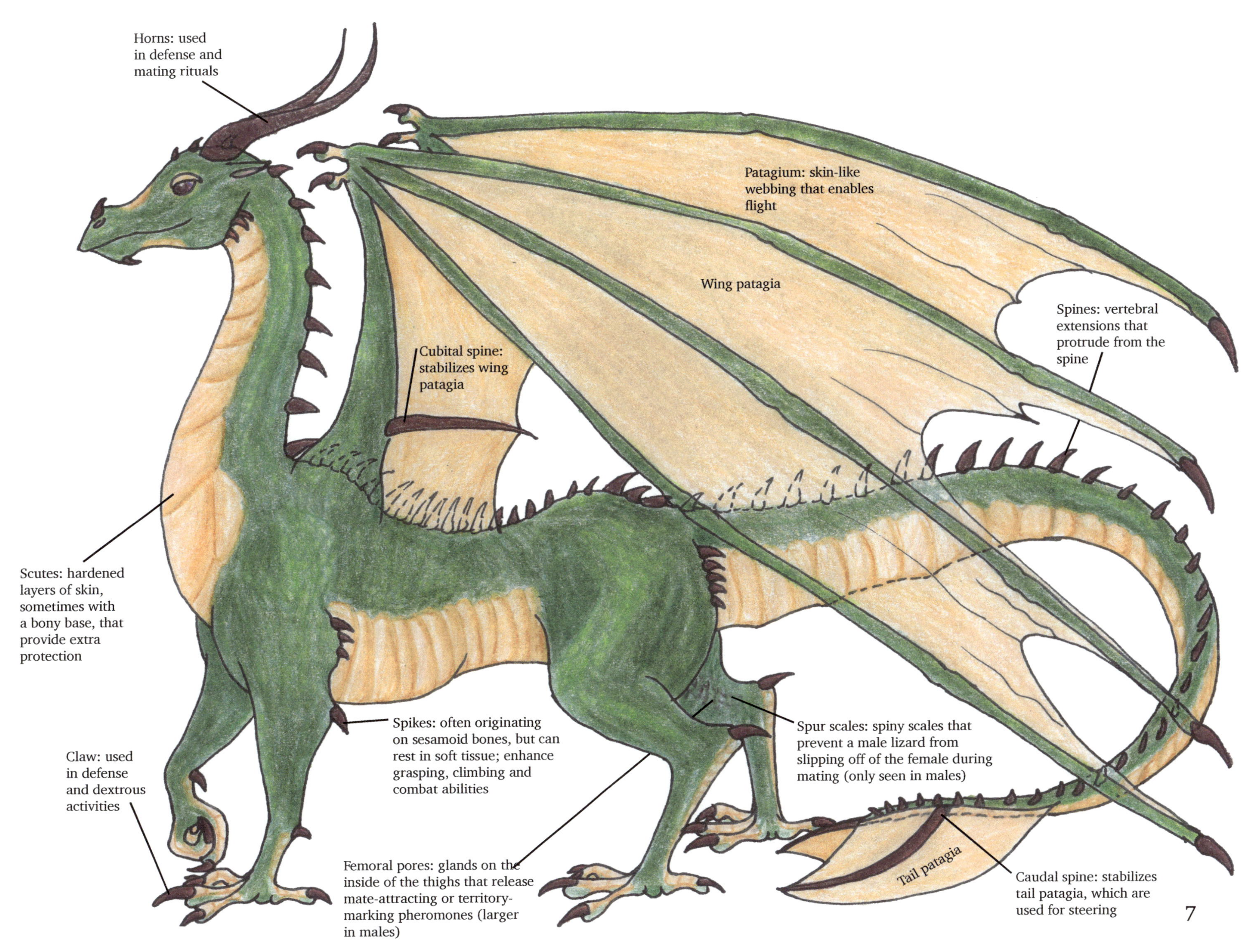

Horns: used in defense and mating rituals
Patagium: skin-like webbing that enables flight
Wing patagia
Spines: vertebral extensions that protrude from the spine
Cubital spine: stabilizes wing patagia
Scutes: hardened layers of skin, sometimes with a bony base, that provide extra protection
Spikes: often originating on sesamoid bones, but can rest in soft tissue; enhance grasping, climbing and combat abilities
Spur scales: spiny scales that prevent a male lizard from slipping off of the female during mating (only seen in males)
Claw: used in defense and dextrous activities
Femoral pores: glands on the inside of the thighs that release mate-attracting or territory-marking pheromones (larger in males)
Tail patagia
Caudal spine: stabilizes tail patagia, which are used for steering

7

A Closer Look at...

The Foot

 *A dragon's foot serves many purposes, from catching food to building nests to maintaining health.*

Why have dragons evolved such large claws?

Immediately apparent is the length of a dragon's claws. Their sharpness is just as extreme. Why have dragon claws evolved into such devastating weapons? Because longer claws were an advantage in many situations. Integral in catching prey, longer claws meant more food and healthier dragons that reproduced more frequently. Not only used for hunting, claws, along with horns and teeth, became more and more prevalent in fighting, whether for food, territory, or a mate. Dragons with better weapons outfought the competition, earning a better chance to reproduce. Thus, through natural selection, the trait of longer, sharper claws became common.

Scutes and Protection

Since a dragon's claws are so important, the foot they are attached to is as well. In order to keep feet in working condition, scutes have spread from being present exclusively on the underside of the body to also covering many areas of the foot. Areas of the foot covered with scutes are usually those exposed to potentially injuring circumstances, such as brush, prey, or other dragons. Thanks to scutes, injury-prone spots such as the tops and bottoms of the toes, the roots of the claws, the base of the foot and the back of the ankle are significantly safer.

Dexterity and the Primitive Thumb

Dexterity is an element seldom seen in reptile feet. Mostly used for scuttling along the ground, reptiles simply need a foot that will propel them forward. Consequently, almost all reptile species have feet incapable of complicated tasks, such as nest building. Birds have feet with a higher level of dexterity, for clinging to tree branches and aiding in the construction of nests, although beaks are often the preferred tool. A dragon's daily tasks require an even higher level of dexterity. Dragons must be able to remove parasites from hard to reach places, grab the fastest, slipperiest prey, and keep nests clean and strong. For these reasons, dragons have developed a primitive opposable thumb, much akin to the toe on the back of a owl's foot that allows it to grasp a tree branch more effectively. This primitive thumb decreases time and increases efficiency of the daily tasks a dragon performs.

Thick Toes

As seen in the cutout of the toe, the bones in the foot are much thicker than one would expect. This increases their strength, in order to withstand the impacts of prey during hunting, or impacts during fighting. Weak bones would shatter, mangling the feet and crippling the dragon, eventually proving fatal.

The Cannon Bone

The bones of the foot are more complex than they seem. The sesamoidal spine sprouts from the heel or wrist, right above the cannon bone. The cannon bone is the result of the fusing of two metatarsals (in the case of the hindleg) or metacarpals (in the case of the foreleg). The cannon bone increases the height and power of the limb, and is also seen in horses, cows, and other ungulates.

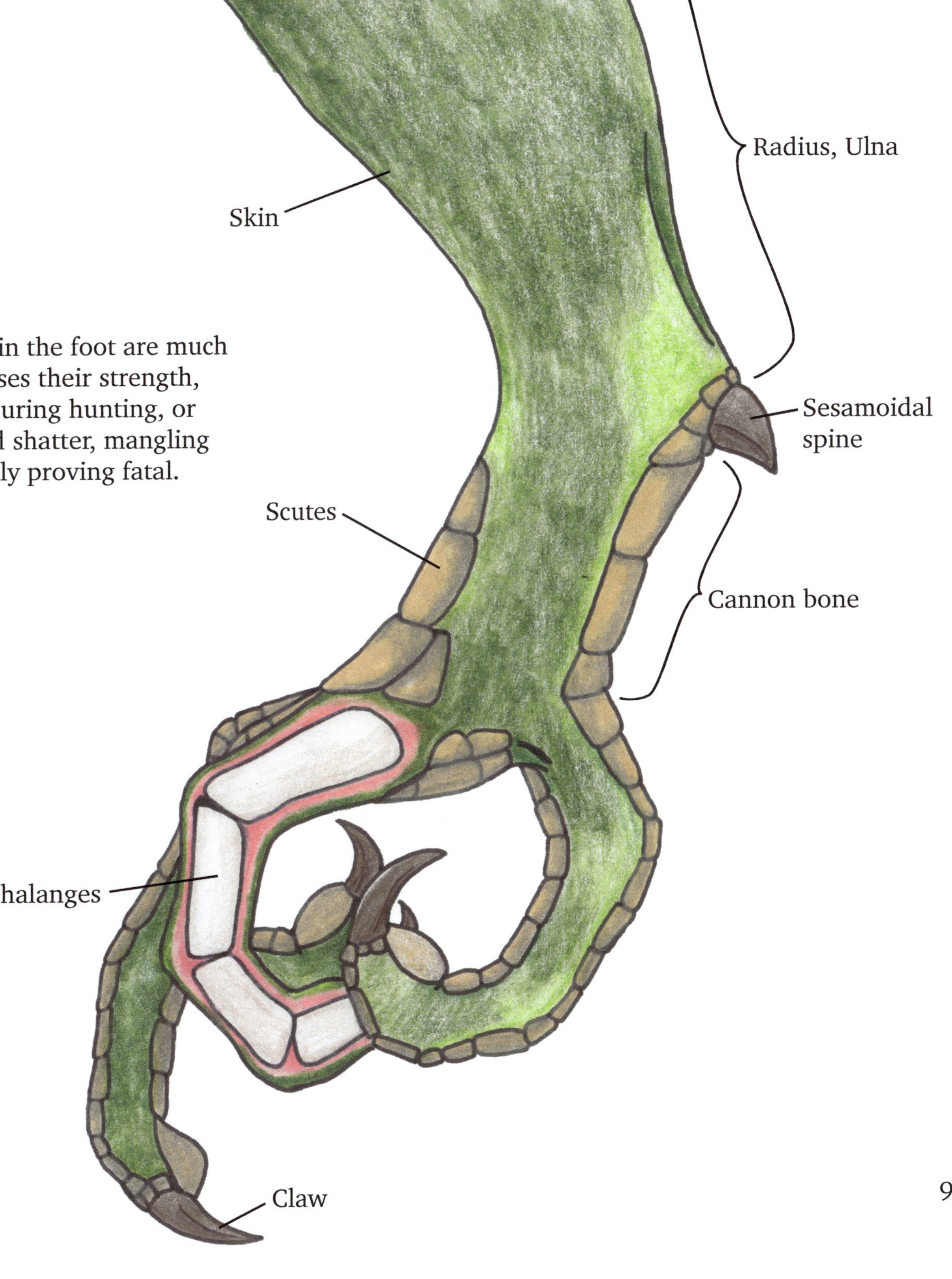

9

A Closer Look at...

The Wings

Initially, although feathered wings seem apt for a dragon, webbed wings prove to be superior.

Why Webbed Wings?

As seen in the table below, feathered wings would have to be so big to support a dragon in flight that the dragon would not be able to carry them! Heavy, cumbersome wings are simply not an option when it comes to survival. Evolution favors other adaptations. Webbed wings, such as those of bats, are more flexible and agile than feathered wings. However, wings comparable to a bat's would also be too big. So we end up at the bottom of the chart: the pterosaurs. Pterosaurs' wings optimized their size, allowing some of the largest species to weigh up to 250 kilograms and have wingspans of around only 13 meters.

Table: Wingspan Feasibility Ratios

Adult dragons weigh around 450 kilograms (1000 pounds). If they had the same wingspan to bodyweight ratio as Arambourgiania philadelphiae, their wingspan would be an enormous 85 feet! However, dragon wings have more surface area than pterosaur wings of equal length. This means that the wingspan of a 450 kg dragon would stretch to about 20 m (60 ft).

Creature (bird, bat, pterosaur)	Wingspan (m) s	Bodyweight (kg) w	s : w Ratio	Dragon wingspan relative to ratio (m)
Barn Swallow	.34	.02	1 : .06	3333.3
Red-tailed Hawk	.6	1.2	1 : 2	100
Harpy Eagle	2	9	1 : 4.5	44.4
California Condor	3	12	1 : 4	50
Wandering Albatross	3	12	1 : 4	50
Egyptian Fruit Bat	.6	.23	1 : .38	526.32
Malayan Flying Fox	1.8	1	1 : .56	357.14
Pteranodon	5.5	23	1 : 4.18	47.85
Quetzalcoatlus northropi	10	200	1 : 20	10
Arambourgiania philadelphiae	13	250	1 : 19	10.53

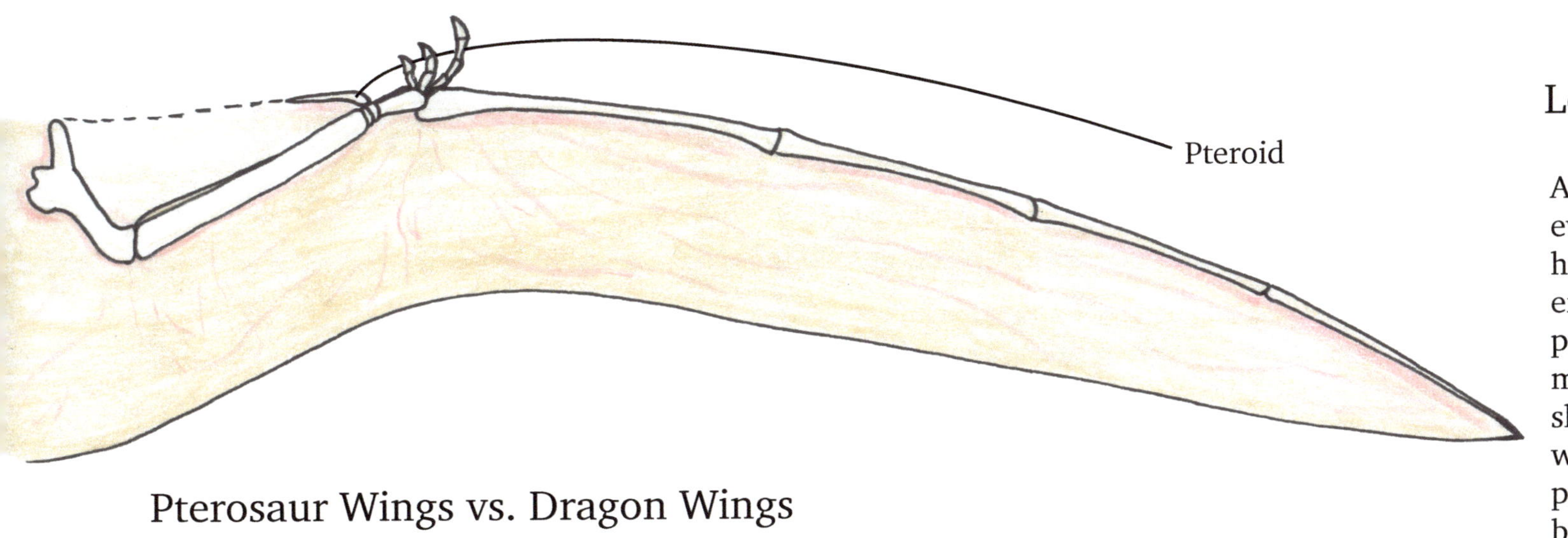

Long-Lost Lineage?

At some point during their evolution, dragons would have had to maximize efficiency just as the pterosaurs did. So it would make sense if dragons shared many characteristics with pterosaurs, as pterosaurs could very well be the ancestors of dragons.

Pterosaur Wings vs. Dragon Wings

A pterosaur wing's structure is largely determined by a lengthened fourth finger, which supports the webbing, or patagium. Pterosaur wings may appear delicate, but are in fact quite strong. Fibers known as actinofibrils run throughout the patagia, strengthening it and preventing tears from spreading. Muscles and tendons are also present in the patagia, allowing for fine adjustments during flight. Pterosaurs also bear a unique bone, the pteroid, that probably aided in supporting the front edges of patagia during flight.

Due to such advantages of webbed wings, it makes sense that dragons would have retained them from their pterosaurian ancestors. However, a few key differences are present. Dragons have three long fingers instead of one; these multiple fingers allow for better control during flight. Dragon patagia do not extend to their tails and feet, as seen in some pterosaurs. Instead they stretch only to the small of the back, allowing for increased mobility on the ground. Elongated sesamoid bones protruding from each elbow–cubital spines–replace the role of the lower legs and tail in stabilizing and extending the wing. The patagia are also responsible for the majority of a dragon's homeostasis, because they cool blood flowing through them.

11

A Closer Look at...

The Pouch

The pouch is a parent's last resort in the case of disaster.

A Roomy Ride

Dragon tails are quite thick, made mostly of muscle. All this muscle provides a significant amount of expendable space that is put to good use by a dragon's pouch. In females tail space is ample, since the reproductive organs are housed in the abdominal cavity. Consequently, male pouches are about half the size of those of females, due to the space taken up by the hemipenes. This also means that females are the primary pouch users. Males typically only use theirs in the case of an emergency relocation.

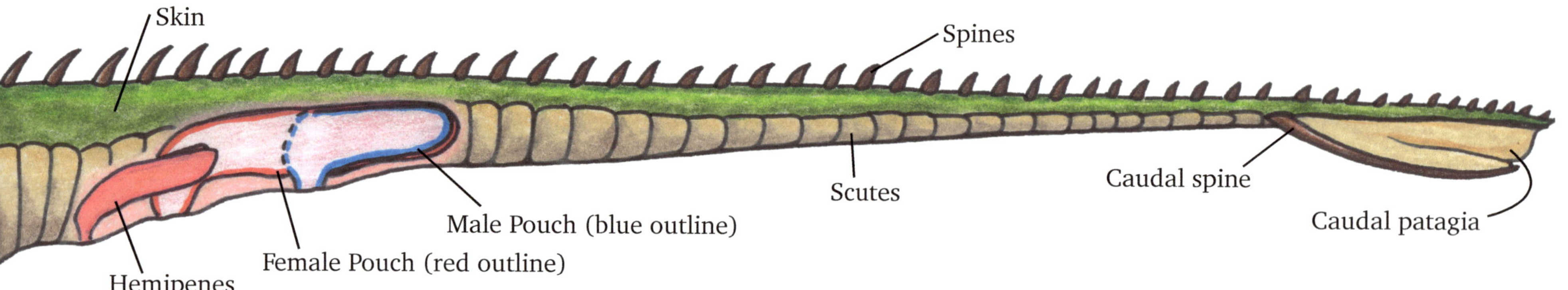

Safety Scutes

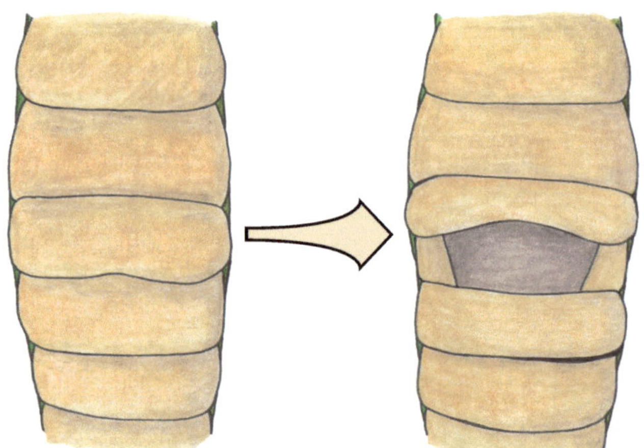

The entry to the pouch is a special scute that slides over its neighbor. By closing back over the pouch once the young have entered, it keeps them protected. The image on the left pictures the pouch scute open, allowing a view into the pouch. Tail pouches may seem dangerous, prone to swinging about and thrashing around, but in reality they are very safe. The base of the tail does not move much, and adults are considerably more cautious when carrying their young.

Saving the Nest

Dragon pouches have multiple purposes. If an event, such as a territory takeover, natural disaster, or epidemic, occurred that caused an emergency evacuation of a nest, pouches would save the day. By providing a safe environment for unhatched eggs, pouches can relocate a dragon's brood. Newly hatched dragons can also fit in pouches; dragons only become too big to fit in a pouch once they are fledged, which negates the use of the pouch anyway. However, a clutch of eggs can only be successfully relocated in one trip by a pair of dragons. Alone, one dragon is unable to carry a clutch or brood; nest survival is unlikely without cooperation. Females have roomier pouches than males, because male reproductive organs take up half of the space needed for a pouch the size of a female's. Females are also statistically larger than males in the majority of reptilian species, including dragons, allotting more tail space.

A Closer Look at...

The Egg

Eggs provide dragons with many advantages, and are a true evolutionary marvel.

Why Eggs?

Why do most reptiles not give live birth? In other words, why are they oviparous (egg-laying) instead of vivaparous (live-birthing)? It has long been debated why creatures became oviparous, but three theories have arisen:

1) Reptiles needed to be able to flee from predators, and the weight of a fully developed fetus slowed them down.

2) The weight of a fully developed infant made flight impossible.

3) Females were physically unable to carry large numbers of fully developed offspring, so laying eggs early increased offspring production.

Overall, the advantages of eggs prevailed, and eggs became the primary reproductive mechanism in reptiles and later birds. Primitive, soft shelled eggs are still laid by creatures such as turtles and pythons, but hard-shelled eggs provide greater protection from external threats, and hence would be laid by dragons.

The Portable Womb

Amniotic eggs are thought to have evolved in prehistoric aquatic creatures, such as early amphibians. The amniotic egg allowed amphibians to colonize land, and is still seen today, in reptiles, turtles, birds and monotremes (such as the echidna). What makes an amniotic egg special are its fluid-filled membranes and hard, protective shell. There are two main membranes: the chorion and the amnion. The chorion surrounds all of the membrane sacs and the embryo, sitting just inside the shell of the egg. It promotes gas exchange between the inside of the egg and the outside environment, but prevents the loss of fluid. It also serves as a barrier to disease. The amnion surrounds the embryo, and is filled with amniotic fluid, which cushions the developing embryo. There are also two membranous sacs: the yolk sac and the allantois. The yolk sac is directly attached to the embryo and contains yolk, nutrients that the embryo uses to fuel its growth. The allantois collects the embryo's waste as it develops, and also aids the chorion in promoting gas exchange. Together, these membranes make an egg an extraordinary portable womb.

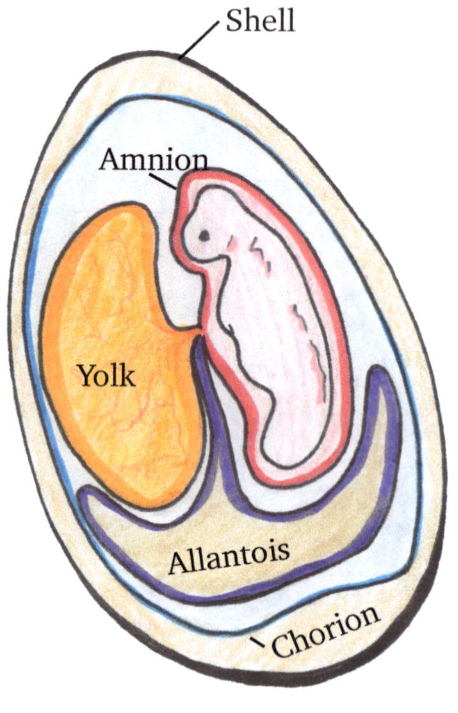

Examining Embryology

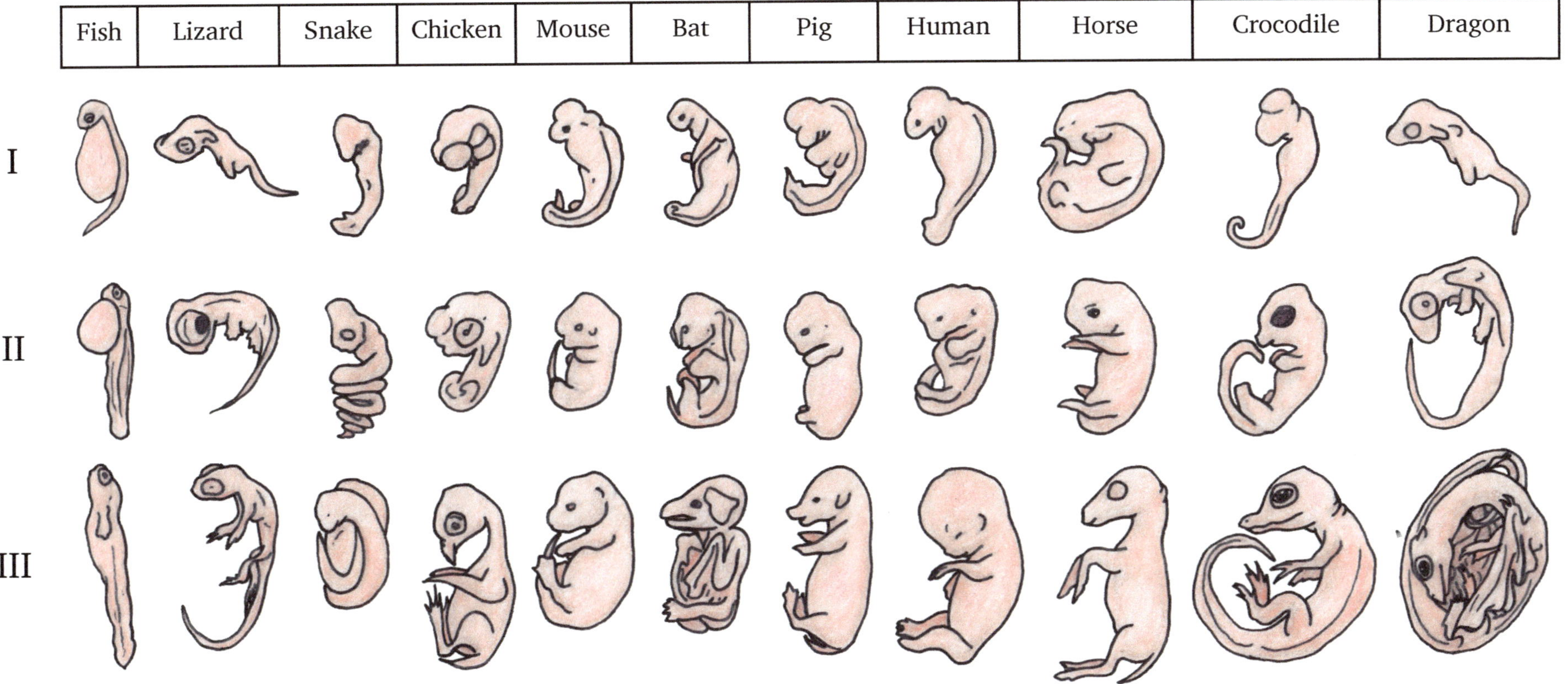

Scientists have learned much about the evolutionary relationships between species, or phylogeny, through the study of embryos. Although an adult mouse and an adult human look nothing alike, their stage I embryos show striking similarities. These similarities indicate that mice and humans have a common ancestor.

Common ancestry can also be implemented in determining the development of a dragon embryo. In the table above, embryos from ten extant (living today) species are compared in stages I, II, and III. By examining the similarities and unique characteristics of each species, a dragon embryo has been pictured for each stage.

In the dragon embryo, notice the similarities to other embryos' characteristics. The dragon's stage I embryo mirrors that of the lizard. The formation and folding of its wings echoes that of a bat's. And the curling that allows it to remain fitting in its egg resembles that of a lizard's, a snake's, a chicken's and a crocodile's.

Altogether, a collection of these shared characteristics shows what species dragons are most closely related to. First, the lizard. Second, the crocodile. Third, the chicken. Fourth, the snake. And fifth, the bat, and other mammals. Although it may seem surprising, all of the species pictured above share a common ancestor.

The Muscles:

An Inside Look

Mighty Muscles

Muscles don't simply move a dragon's body parts–they hold together the skeleton and serve as connective tissue all throughout the body. Muscles also generate heat during movement, which a dragon makes good use of in the case of cold spells. Thick skin insulates their body, helping to keep heat in. If they need to cool off, they pump more blood through their patagia, where it loses excess heat to the environment.

Besides warming a dragon up, muscles are of course necessary for movement. They facilitate not only the workings of the external body parts, but the internal organs as well. Cardiac muscle pumps away in the heart, while smooth muscle moves food through the intestines. Skeletal muscle covers the skeleton and moves the limbs. The stronger the skeletal muscles, the stronger the dragon. And since stronger dragons have better chances of finding food, winning fights and reproducing, the majority of dragons appear very muscly. Only the fittest survive, and these three types of muscle keep a dragon alive.

Diagram Details

The diagram to the right may look like a tangle of rainbows, but the colors are actually a guide. In general, muscles on certain body parts aid in the movement of those parts. However, certain muscles have different uses. The transversospinalis, for example, does not move the spine. Instead, it covers the spine, serving as a protective layer of insulation. The tongue does not move any significant body part. It moves food around in the mouth.

In the diagram, muscles with common purposes in the same area are often the same colors. For example, in the forearms and wings, muscle colors match exactly because they share both a name and a purpose. The color schemes match to indicate that all of the muscles in that color scheme work towards a common goal–here, it is moving the forelimbs.

Note that although the fingers of the wings are covered in a thin muscle, it does not serve to move them. It serves as an attachment point for other muscles and tendons strung throughout the patagia of the wings.

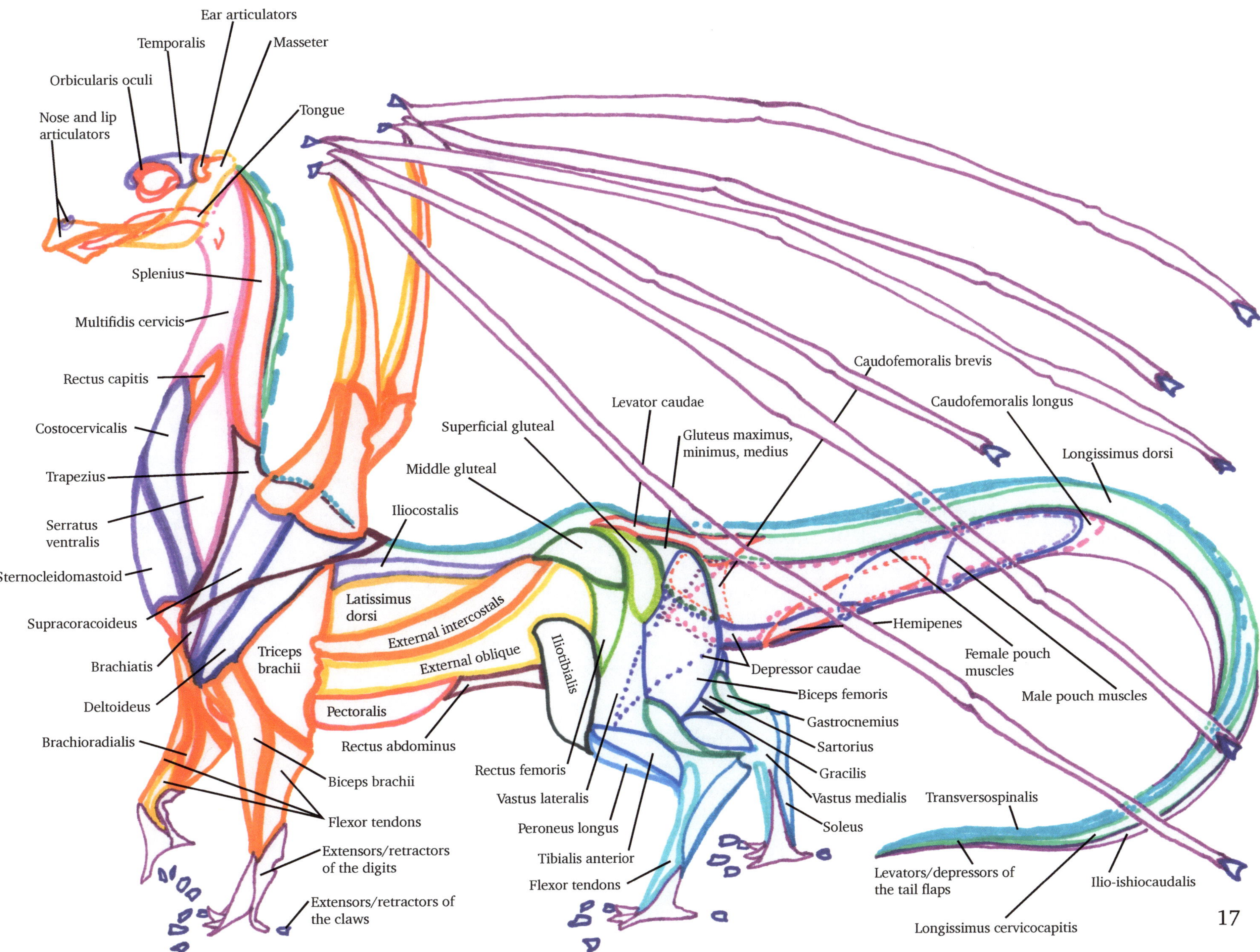

Nose and lip articulators
Orbicularis oculi
Temporalis
Ear articulators
Masseter
Tongue
Splenius
Multifidis cervicis
Rectus capitis
Costocervicalis
Trapezius
Serratus ventralis
Sternocleidomastoid
Supracoracoideus
Brachiatis
Deltoideus
Brachioradialis
Triceps brachii
Latissimus dorsi
External intercostals
External oblique
Iliotibialis
Pectoralis
Rectus abdominus
Biceps brachii
Flexor tendons
Extensors/retractors of the digits
Extensors/retractors of the claws
Superficial gluteal
Middle gluteal
Iliocostalis
Rectus femoris
Vastus lateralis
Peroneus longus
Tibialis anterior
Flexor tendons
Levator caudae
Gluteus maximus, minimus, medius
Caudofemoralis brevis
Caudofemoralis longus
Longissimus dorsi
Hemipenes
Depressor caudae
Biceps femoris
Gastrocnemius
Sartorius
Gracilis
Vastus medialis
Soleus
Female pouch muscles
Male pouch muscles
Transversospinalis
Levators/depressors of the tail flaps
Ilio-ishiocaudalis
Longissimus cervicocapitis

A Closer Look at...

The Cardiovascular and Respiratory Systems

The Journey of Blood

Dragon blood serves the same purposes as ours: circulating oxygen and nutrients. It wouldn't be a different color or have magical properties, but its constant journey is remarkable. Blood is pumped through the body by the heart, which along with the blood vessels forms the cardiovascular system. The respiratory system brings oxygen into the body. How do these two systems interact? It all starts with a deep breath. Fresh air flows into the lungs and air sacs, and the lungs busy themselves absorbing oxygen. Thinly membraned alveoli-like sacs bring blood so close to air that it absorbs oxygen and rids itself of carbon dioxide. The oxygen rich blood (red) then enters the left atrium of the heart through the pulmonary veins. The heart pumps it into the main ventricle and out through the aortas. The left systemic aorta carries richly oxygenated blood to demanding areas of the body, such as the muscles. The right systemic aorta conserves oxygen by diverting poorly oxygenated blood to less demanding areas, such as the stomach. Both aortas carry blood into the body, where it disperses through vast networks of vessels. Blood returning from the body is deoxygenated (blue); it left its oxygen in the cells it travelled to. Now the blood must become oxygenated again. Lungs to the rescue! Deoxygenated blood enters the heart through the sinus venosus. This hearty vein carries it into the right atrium. Then it flows into the lower ventricle and out to the lungs through the pulmonary arteries. The blood absorbs oxygen in the lungs and re-enters the heart to be pumped back through the body, starting the cycle again.

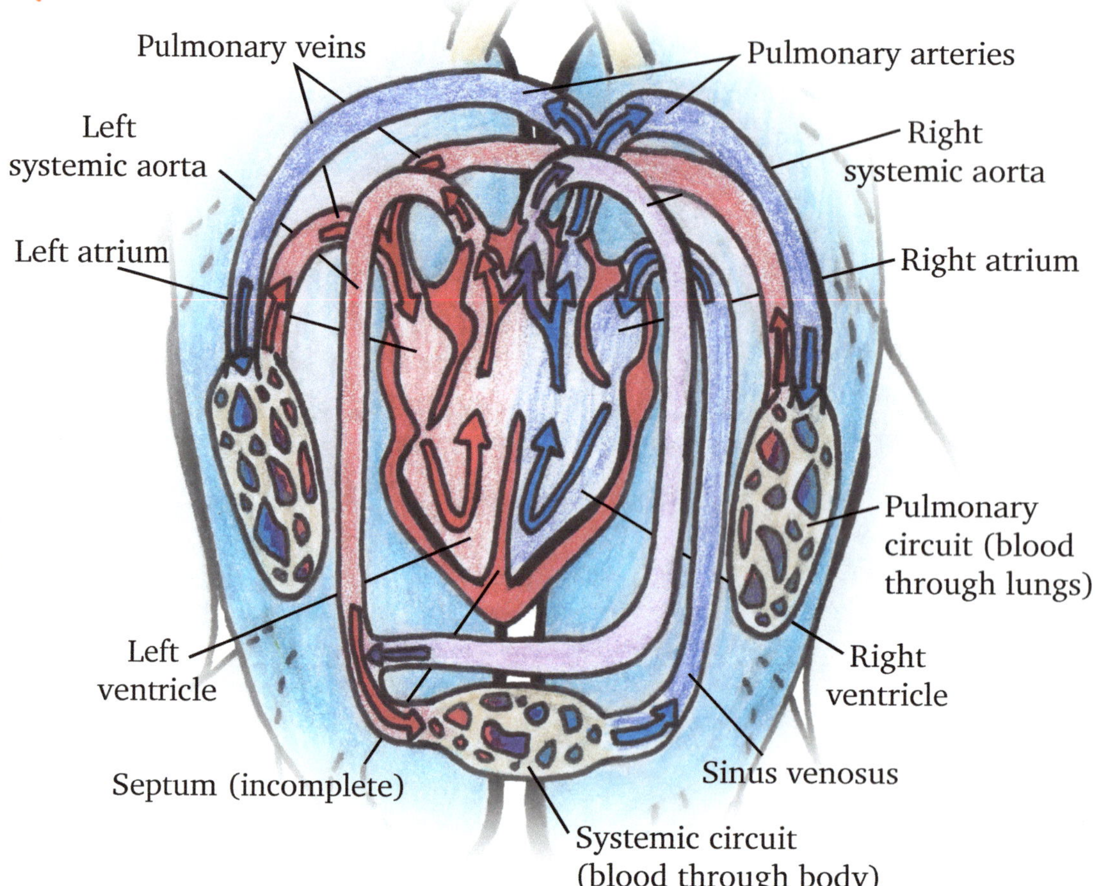

The respiratory system partners with the cardiovascular system to circulate oxygen and nutrients throughout the body.

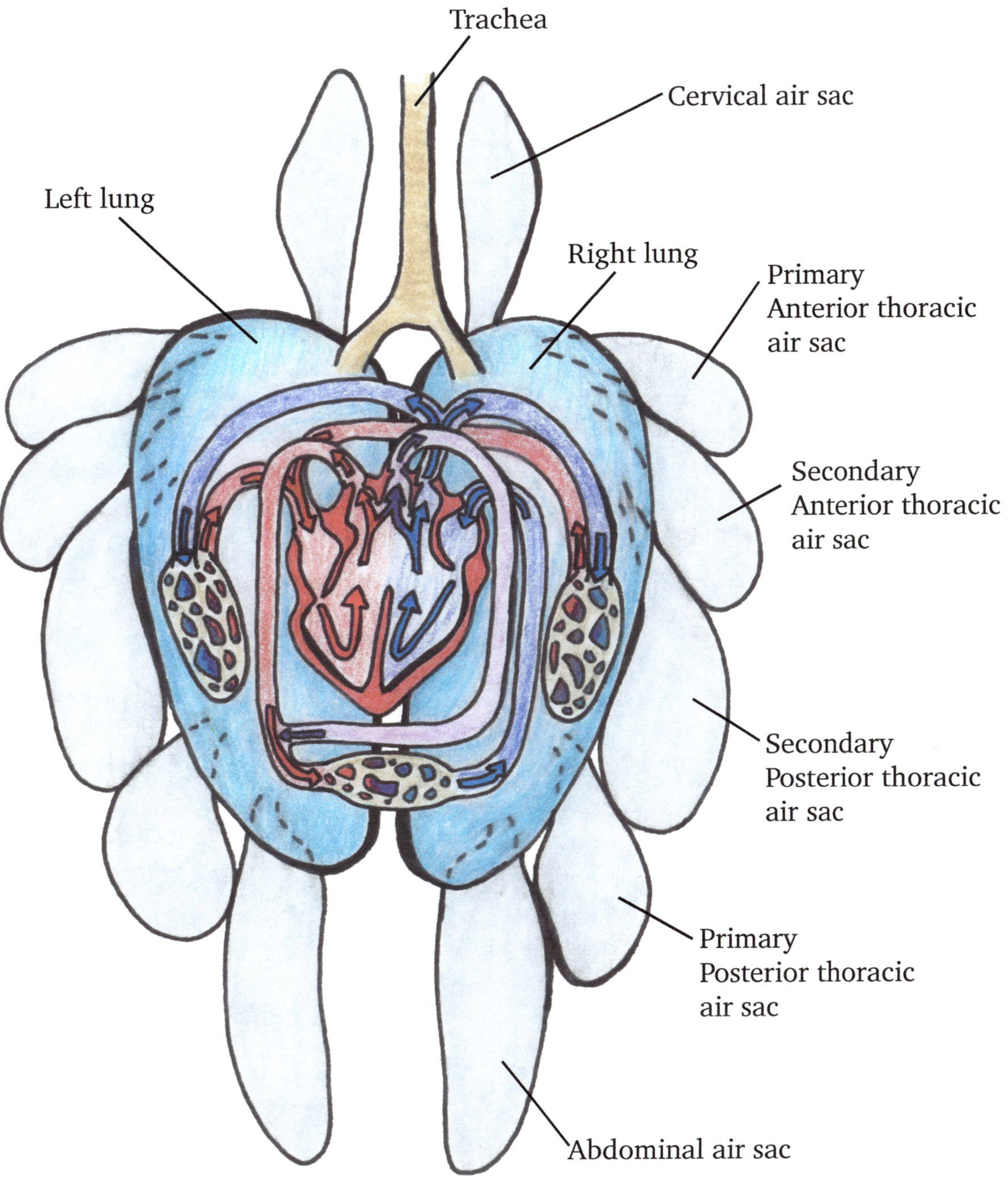

Amazing Air Sacs

Dragon lungs resemble bird lungs, which look nothing like mammalian lungs, aside from the actual lung itself. The defining difference is the presence of air sacs. Air sacs are unable to absorb oxygen. Instead, they store fresh air that is inhaled until exhalation. When a bird inhales, its air sacs and lungs fill with air. The lungs absorb oxygen from the fresh air, and the air sacs hold steady. When the bird exhales, the stale air is pushed out of its lungs and the still fresh air from the air sacs is pushed into the lungs. Now, the lungs absorb oxygen again. Thanks to a series of air sacs, birds can oxygenate their blood while inhaling and exhaling, which mammals are unable to do. By absorbing oxygen on both strokes, birds have maximized efficiency while in the air, delivering more oxygen to flight muscles and thus increasing performance of those muscles.

The Skeleton:

An Inside Look

Bones of the Beast

Bones have many important qualities. First of all, they are strong, supporting a dragon throughout its life. Secondly, many grooves, nicks and holes are present on bones that allow muscles, tendons, and other connective tissue to knit themselves into and onto the skeleton. A spongy (not hollow) bone center lightens the bones, allowing for flight. Specialized bones protect organs. The ribs protect the trachea and esophagus in the neck, organs in the abdominal cavity, and pouches in the tail. Furthermore, the bones play a vital role in the immune system. Bones contain marrow that produces many types of blood cells, including red blood cells. Their production of such blood cells keeps a dragon healthy and disease resistant.

The Super Sesamoid

Dragons' legs are integral to their lives, and injury to one can prove fatal. Hyperextension, an over straightening of a joint, can stretch or even break key tendons and ligaments. Hyperextension in the knee would result if the knee extended all of the way and then some, bending unnaturally forward. The skeleton has a solution: sesamoid bones. Sesamoid bones are found in many joints, providing strong attachment points for muscles and tendons that prevent joint injuries like hyperextension. Prominent sesamoid bones include the patella (kneecap) and calcaneus (heel bone). Other sesamoid bones can be seen where a spine is present, since joint spines originate on sesamoids.

Diagram Details

The colors in the diagram are a guide. They signal relationships between bones. If bones are the same color, they serve the same purpose (e.g. the humerus) or work together (e.g. the cervical vertebrae). Likewise, if bones share a color scheme, they interact to make up specific parts of the body. For example, all of the bones in the hindlimbs are cool-colored, indicating that all of those bones together make up the hindlimbs.

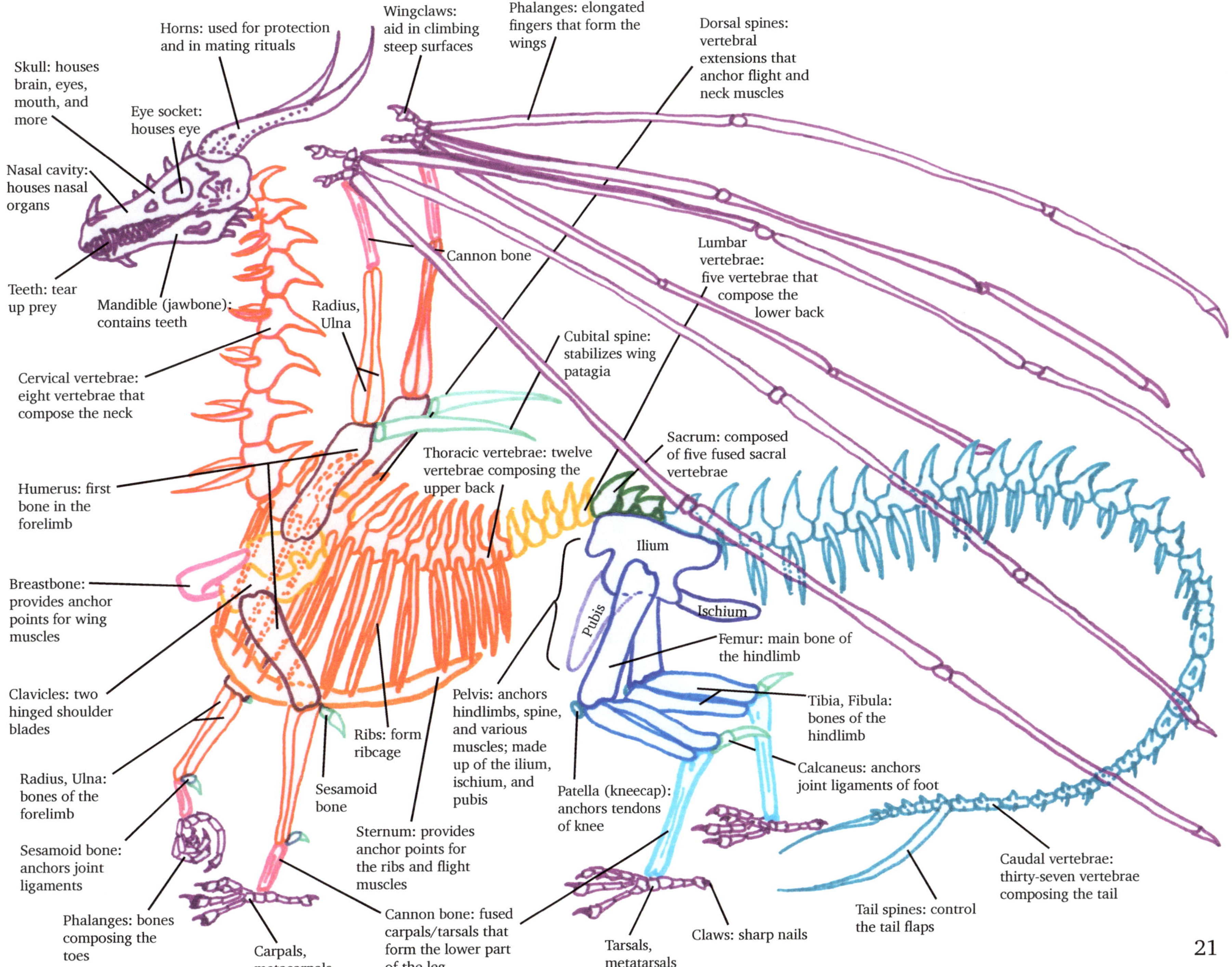

Skull: houses brain, eyes, mouth, and more
Horns: used for protection and in mating rituals
Wingclaws: aid in climbing steep surfaces
Phalanges: elongated fingers that form the wings
Dorsal spines: vertebral extensions that anchor flight and neck muscles
Eye socket: houses eye
Nasal cavity: houses nasal organs
Cannon bone
Lumbar vertebrae: five vertebrae that compose the lower back
Teeth: tear up prey
Mandible (jawbone): contains teeth
Radius, Ulna
Cubital spine: stabilizes wing patagia
Cervical vertebrae: eight vertebrae that compose the neck
Thoracic vertebrae: twelve vertebrae composing the upper back
Sacrum: composed of five fused sacral vertebrae
Humerus: first bone in the forelimb
Ilium
Breastbone: provides anchor points for wing muscles
Pubis
Ischium
Femur: main bone of the hindlimb
Clavicles: two hinged shoulder blades
Pelvis: anchors hindlimbs, spine, and various muscles; made up of the ilium, ischium, and pubis
Tibia, Fibula: bones of the hindlimb
Radius, Ulna: bones of the forelimb
Ribs: form ribcage
Calcaneus: anchors joint ligaments of foot
Sesamoid bone: anchors joint ligaments
Sesamoid bone
Patella (kneecap): anchors tendons of knee
Phalanges: bones composing the toes
Carpals, metacarpals
Sternum: provides anchor points for the ribs and flight muscles
Cannon bone: fused carpals/tarsals that form the lower part of the leg
Tarsals, metatarsals
Claws: sharp nails
Tail spines: control the tail flaps
Caudal vertebrae: thirty-seven vertebrae composing the tail

21

A Closer Look at...

The Skull and Brain

Looking In

Diagram Details

The dragon brain is composed of five
main sections: the cerebral hemisphere
(red), cerebellum (blue), optic lobes
(yellow), olfactory lobe (olive green),
and medulla and brain stem (violet).
Each section of the brain plays an
important role in daily life.

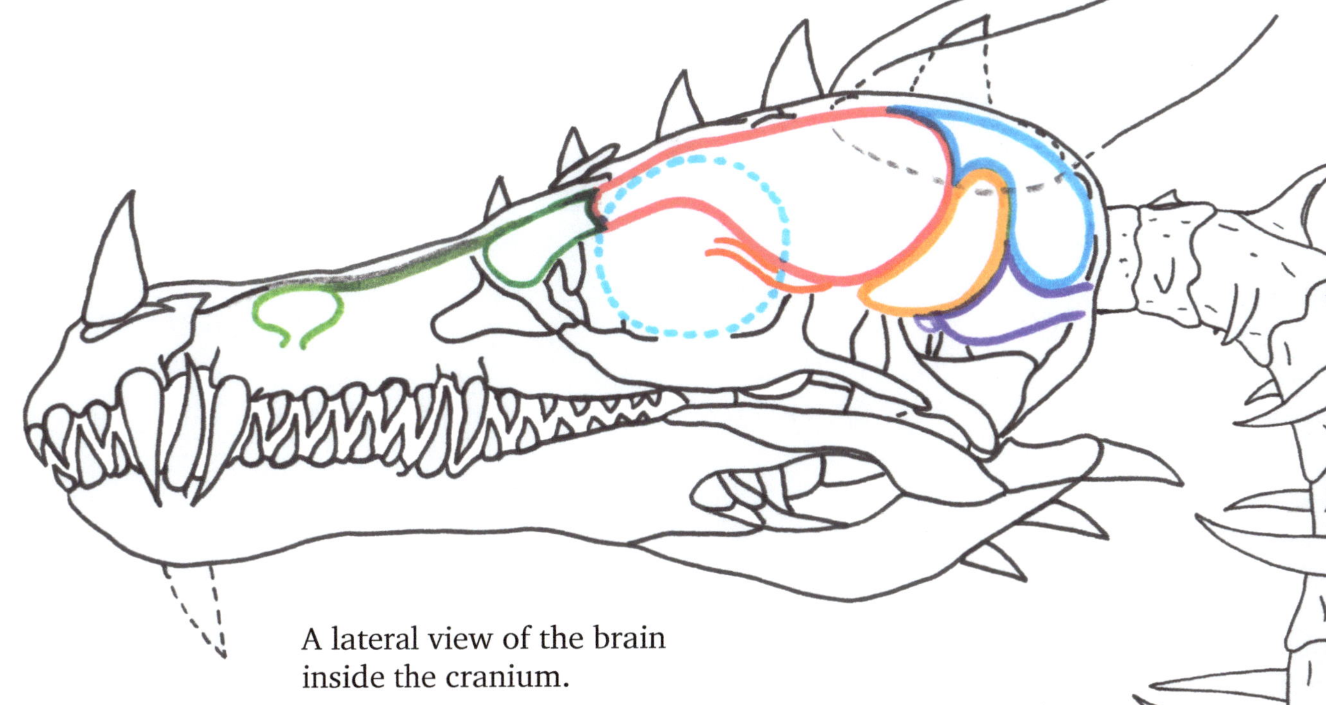

A lateral view of the brain
inside the cranium.

Brainpower

The cerebral hemisphere contains many complexities, but its involvement in behavioral instincts and learned
intelligence is particularly significant. It also has a hand in reasoning, fine motor skills and interpretation of
sensory input. The cerebellum specializes in the involuntary side of operations. It maintains balance, posture,
and coordinates muscle movements. Optic lobes link directly to the optic nerves, processing multitudes of visual
information from the eyes. The chiasma is a point where the optic nerves slightly intertwine as they cross over
each other. Smell is up to the olfactory lobe, a lobe projecting towards the edge of the nasal cavity. It also sprouts a
nerve that connects it to the vomeronasal, or Jacobson's, organ. The brain stem relays information from the rest of
the brain to the spinal cord, and also regulates and initiates involuntary bodily functions such as digestion, sleep,
heart rate, breathing and body temperature.

The brain sits inside the cranium (the skull), protected by a thick layer of bone. The brain is a particularly delicate
organ, however, and if knocked too hard can result in a concussion. Fluid build-up on the surface of the brain can
cut off access to the spinal cord via the brain stem, and a pinched brain stem is almost certainly fatal. So it makes
sense that dragons are protective of their heads; amidst all of those fearsome horns and teeth is a fragile mind.

The Organs:

An Inside Look

Organ System Secrets

Dragons have the essentials: a digestive system, a circulatory system, a respiratory system, a reproductive system, a nervous system… you get the idea. However, they possess some unfamiliar yet truly remarkable organs.

In the digestive system, there are two crops. As in birds, a dragon's primary crop serves as a storage unit for excess food. It also plays a key role in raising their young, by secreting a fatty, protein-rich substance known as "crop milk." Although crop milk is not true milk, like that of mammals, it serves the same purpose: nurturing helpless young. Crop milk also contains red and white blood cells from the parent, kickstarting the chick's immune system. The secondary crop serves only to secrete crop milk.

In the circulatory and respiratory systems, there are the lungs. They sure look a lot different from human lungs! But the lungs themselves, in the center of all those air sacs, are the same. They still oxygenate the blood. However, unlike creatures without air sacs that only absorb oxygen while inhaling, dragons absorb oxygen while exhaling too. Seen most prominently in birds, air sacs increase a bird's efficiency in the air; flight requires lots of muscle activity, and thus oxygen too. Serving the same purpose in dragons, they are a genius way to solve the flight efficiency issue.

Brainiacs?

The nervous system has a special characteristic: the size of the brain. Unlike most reptile brains, which are relatively small compared to their individuals' body sizes, dragon brains are relatively large. And also unlike most reptile brains, which have an underdeveloped cerebral hemisphere, dragons have a moderately developed one, providing them with higher, more complex thought. Much is still unknown about the brain.

Reproductive Superpowers

The reproductive system also contains hidden features. Males sport a hemipenis, a forked penis that allows more frequent copulation. A male ready to breed more often has a better chance of successfully reproducing. It also ensures that if one side of the hemipenis becomes injured, the other can compensate. Snakes and lizards have hemipenes, and most are species-specific. Star-like and spine-like projections prevent cross-breeding of distinct species, keeping populations healthy. Female dragons have a trick up their sleeve too: they can store sperm from numerous males for years at a time. It is still unknown exactly how certain female reptiles are able to do this, but recent research is suggesting that tubular structures in the female reproductive tract, sperm storage tubules (SSTs), definitely play the major part.

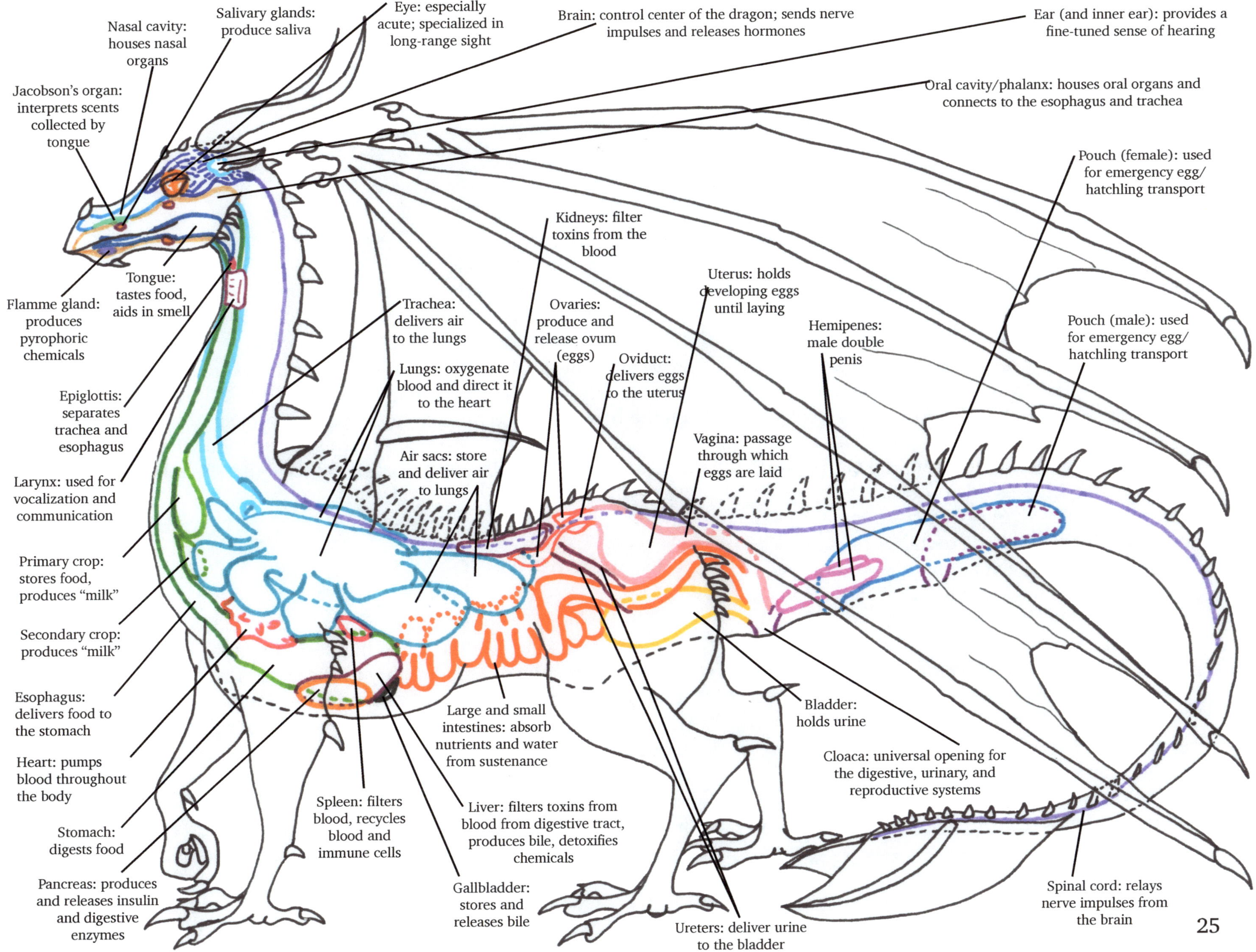

Nasal cavity: houses nasal organs
Salivary glands: produce saliva
Eye: especially acute; specialized in long-range sight
Brain: control center of the dragon; sends nerve impulses and releases hormones
Ear (and inner ear): provides a fine-tuned sense of hearing
Jacobson's organ: interprets scents collected by tongue
Oral cavity/phalanx: houses oral organs and connects to the esophagus and trachea
Pouch (female): used for emergency egg/hatchling transport
Tongue: tastes food, aids in smell
Kidneys: filter toxins from the blood
Flamme gland: produces pyrophoric chemicals
Uterus: holds developing eggs until laying
Pouch (male): used for emergency egg/hatchling transport
Epiglottis: separates trachea and esophagus
Trachea: delivers air to the lungs
Ovaries: produce and release ovum (eggs)
Oviduct: delivers eggs to the uterus
Hemipenes: male double penis
Larynx: used for vocalization and communication
Lungs: oxygenate blood and direct it to the heart
Vagina: passage through which eggs are laid
Air sacs: store and deliver air to lungs
Primary crop: stores food, produces "milk"
Secondary crop: produces "milk"
Esophagus: delivers food to the stomach
Large and small intestines: absorb nutrients and water from sustenance
Bladder: holds urine
Heart: pumps blood throughout the body
Cloaca: universal opening for the digestive, urinary, and reproductive systems
Stomach: digests food
Spleen: filters blood, recycles blood and immune cells
Liver: filters toxins from blood from digestive tract, produces bile, detoxifies chemicals
Pancreas: produces and releases insulin and digestive enzymes
Gallbladder: stores and releases bile
Ureters: deliver urine to the bladder
Spinal cord: relays nerve impulses from the brain

25

A Closer Look at...

The Mouth

Parts of the Mouth

Such an intimidating mouth does indeed contain more than teeth. Other oral organs are integral to a dragon's survival. The tongue not only specializes in taste, allowing a dragon to determine whether a food is edible or toxic, but also comprises a significant portion of a dragon's sense of smell. The forked shape of the tongue, reminiscent of a snake's, allows it to pick up scent molecules from the air. Flicking of the tongue initiates this process. The tongue goes out into the air, picks up scent molecules, and retreats back into the mouth. Contrary to common belief, such a tongue does not allow reptiles to literally taste the air. Instead, once returned to the mouth, the tip of the tongue slides into a recess in the roof of the mouth. This recess is the vomeronasal organ, commonly known as the Jacobson's organ. The vomeronasal organ interprets the scent molecules delivered by the tongue, transferring the information to the dragon's brain via a nerve connecting it to the olfactory lobe. The blue color of the tongue protects it from sunburn, since it is constantly exposed to the sun during all of that flicking.

Terrible Teeth

Teeth grow from the bones of the mandible and skull. All of the teeth are thecodont teeth, which, unlike human teeth, replace themselves when lost. They grow right back in the same socket. So that small gap this male has in his upper right row of teeth is no big deal–a new tooth is already emerging. Notice the three pairs of fangs: two pairs on top, one snuggled in between them on the bottom. These long fangs keep prey from slipping out of a dragon's grasp, while the other teeth slice up food. Together, a dragon's teeth-a full set numbering 66 total-are the key to a successful kill.

The Flamme Gland

Notice the slight lump in front of the tongue. This fleshy mass is the flamme gland. As the name implies, the flamme gland is responsible for the dragon's ability to "breathe" fire. Yet again, dragons are not able to literally breathe fire, as many think. Their ability is actually thanks to the pyrophoric substances produced by the flamme gland. Pyrophoric substances are those that spontaneously ignite when contacting oxygen. So, instead of breathing fire (living tissues would be unable to withstand such heat), dragons spray a cocktail of pyrophoric chemicals from their flamme gland to produce the drastic infernos that they are associated with.

Smaller horns (spikes) grown around the head provide further protection. Spikes on the back of the jawbone shield the neck and throat. Spikes on top of the head and surrounding the eyes protect the eyes. On the top and bottom of the snout, spikes defend the nostrils and lips.

Scutes are hardened layers of skin that are extremely strong, yet flexible. They overlap each other at points of common movement, such as the neck and tail. On the head, they are less mobile, acting more as a helmet. They cover the vulnerable top of the head and underside of the jaw, which would prove fatal if injured. In most dragons, scutes are the same color, but in fact can range in color from a light tan to a deep brown. A dragon's scute color is determined by its environment, further bolstering its camouflage.

Horns are sleek, strong, and sharp, providing a very effective defense and deterrent for any foolish creature attempting to harm a dragon. Besides as weapons, horns are also used in mating displays, shows of strength and prowess that determine one's mate. A new ring of horn is deposited each year, so longer horns mean an older dragon.

A Closer Look at...

The Eye

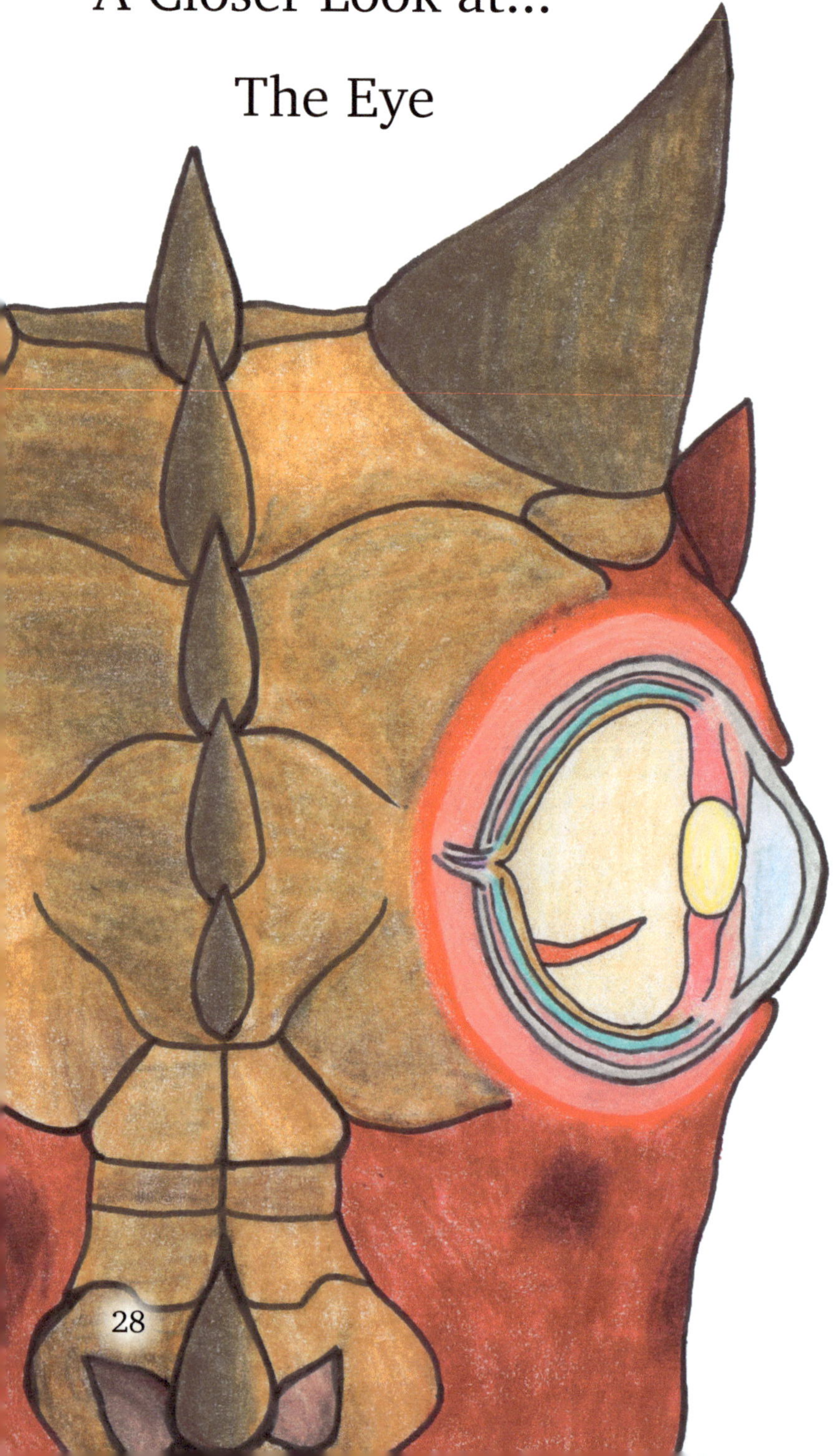

How the Eye Works

The eye is an organic camera, making sense of light with the help of the brain. Let's take a look at how it works by following light through the eye:

1) The iris senses a change in brightness and the dilator pupillae enlarges the pupil to take in more light, or the sphincter pupillae constricts the pupil to take in less light.

2) The cornea reflects the light through the pupil.

3) The lens focuses on the object the dragon is looking at, refracting the light onto the retina so that the image of the object is focused.

4) If it is dark, the tapetum lucidum bounces the light back to the lens, where it is reflected back onto the retina, improving night vision.

5) Light contacts the retina, activating color-sensitive cone cells and light-sensitive rod cells. The fovea, the very center of the macula (which is the center of the retina), contains a vastly greater percentage of these cells, focusing the details of the image.

6) Signals from the rod and cone cells are transmitted to the optic nerve by a thin network of nerves lying just behind the retina, the ganglion cells.

7) The optic nerve transmits the signals through the chiasma to the optic lobes of the brain.

8) The brain interprets the image, flipping it right-side-up and completing the process of sight.

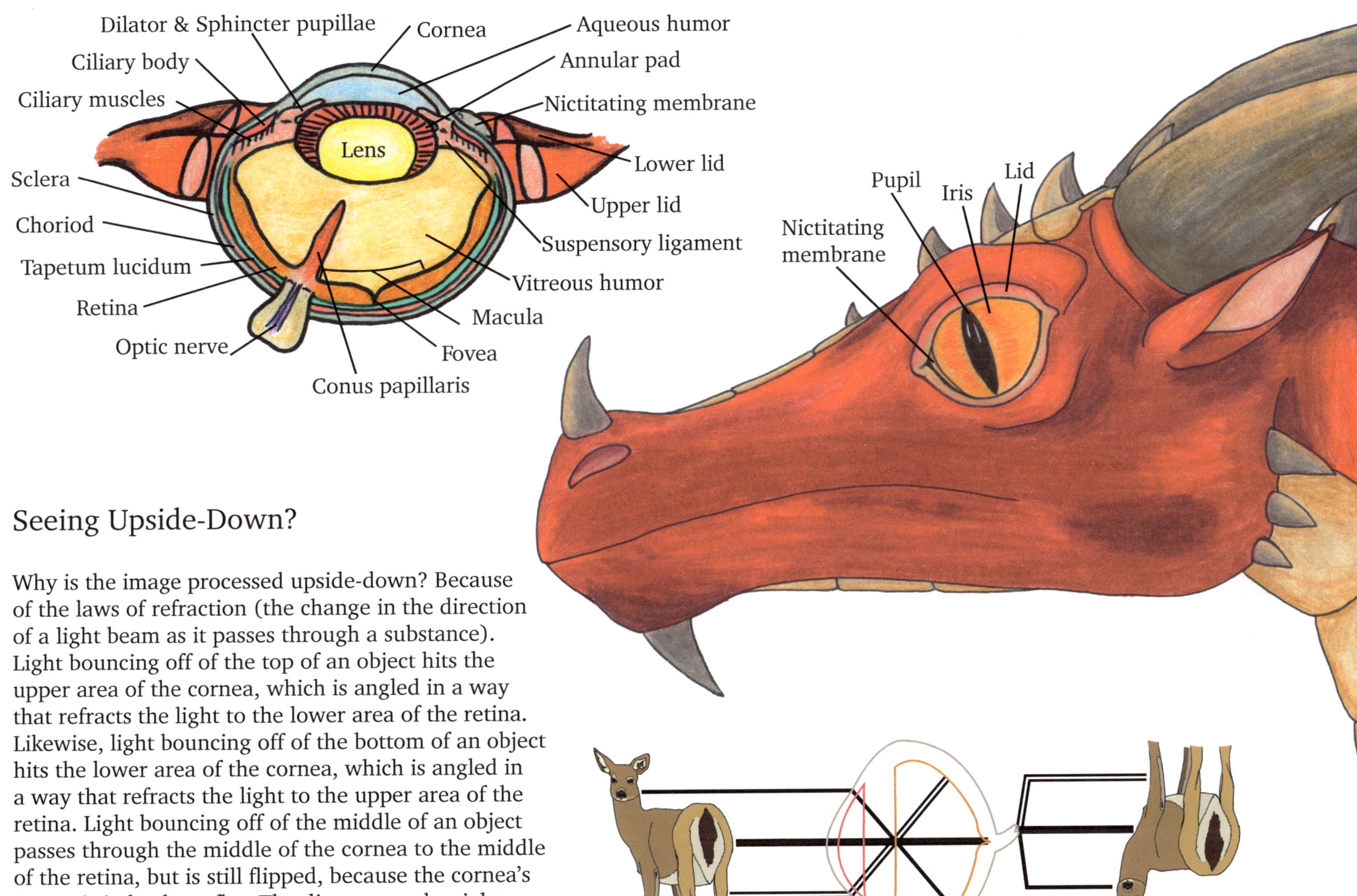

Seeing Upside-Down?

Why is the image processed upside-down? Because of the laws of refraction (the change in the direction of a light beam as it passes through a substance). Light bouncing off of the top of an object hits the upper area of the cornea, which is angled in a way that refracts the light to the lower area of the retina. Likewise, light bouncing off of the bottom of an object hits the lower area of the cornea, which is angled in a way that refracts the light to the upper area of the retina. Light bouncing off of the middle of an object passes through the middle of the cornea to the middle of the retina, but is still flipped, because the cornea's center is indeed not flat. The diagram to the right illustrates this process.

A Closer Look at...

The Ear

The dragon's ear is a surprisingly accurate piece of evolution that dragons could not live without.

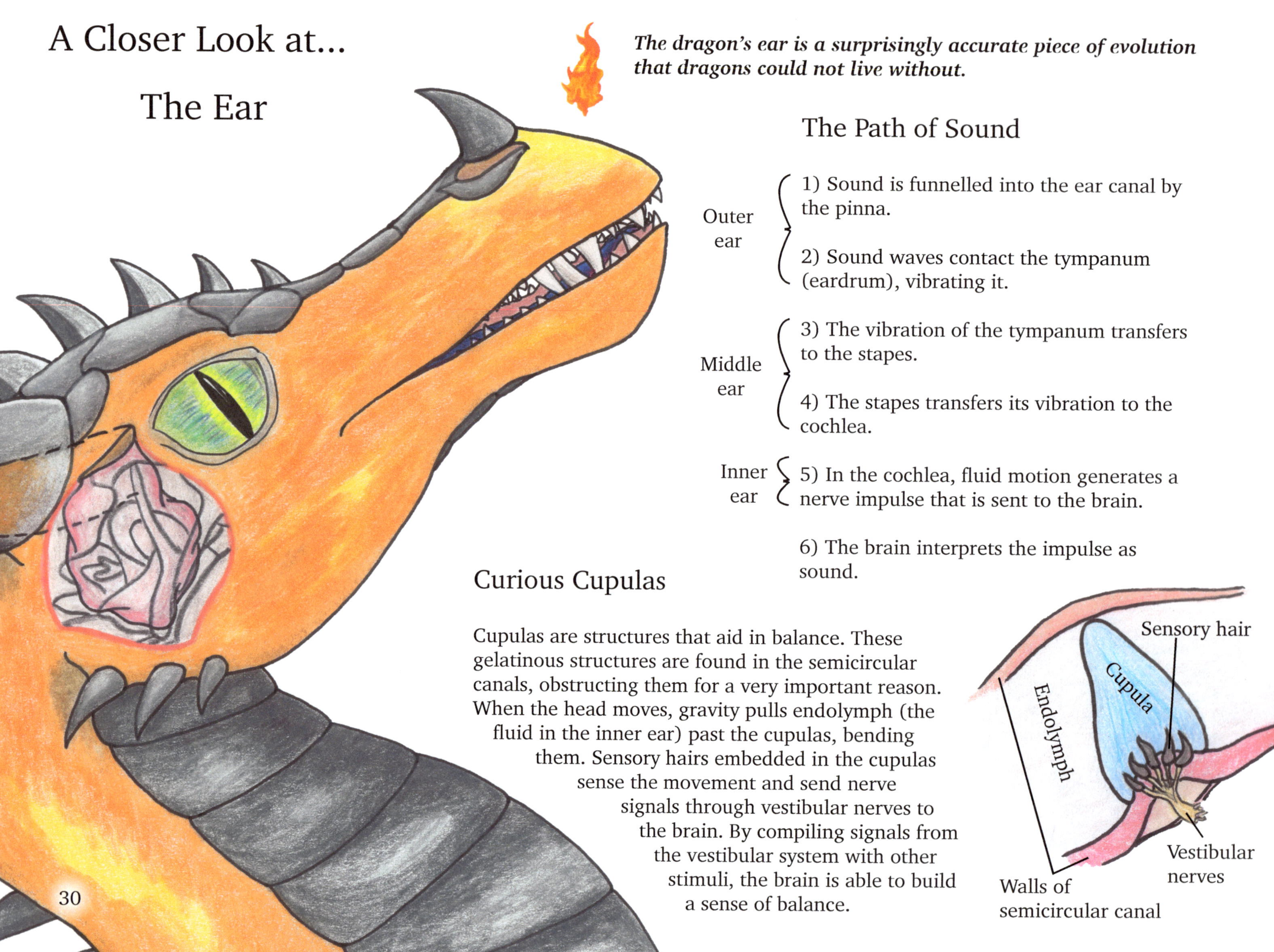

The Path of Sound

Outer ear

1) Sound is funnelled into the ear canal by the pinna.

2) Sound waves contact the tympanum (eardrum), vibrating it.

Middle ear

3) The vibration of the tympanum transfers to the stapes.

4) The stapes transfers its vibration to the cochlea.

Inner ear

5) In the cochlea, fluid motion generates a nerve impulse that is sent to the brain.

6) The brain interprets the impulse as sound.

Curious Cupulas

Cupulas are structures that aid in balance. These gelatinous structures are found in the semicircular canals, obstructing them for a very important reason. When the head moves, gravity pulls endolymph (the fluid in the inner ear) past the cupulas, bending them. Sensory hairs embedded in the cupulas sense the movement and send nerve signals through vestibular nerves to the brain. By compiling signals from the vestibular system with other stimuli, the brain is able to build a sense of balance.

Intriguing Inner Ear

This cluster of canals and chambers looks alien! But it is actually the middle ear. The middle ear has two main purposes: it interprets vibrations as sound and provides a sense of balance. The cochlea is responsible for interpreting sound waves. It then sends these sound signals to the brain via the auditory nerve, and the brain reads them as sound. Balance is all thanks to the semicircular canal system. The anterior, posterior, and lateral semicircular canals sense motion on the yaw, pitch, and roll axes. Neither one of the three canals sense motion on one axis; instead, they work together. All three connect to the utricle, which senses horizontal motion. The saccule senses vertical motion. Altogether, the inner ear is an extremely important part of the dragon. It keeps the dragon oriented, especially during flight, and picks up the slightest sounds during the hunt.

Captivating Qualities

Shown in the full head picture to the left is the auditory cavity, which houses the delicate structures of the ear. The diagram to the right illustrates the inside of the auditory cavity. These structures require protection because of their fragile nature. The eardrum is vulnerable to tears or punctures, the ear canal to infection, the cochlea to damage from excess noise. However, evolution has solved these problems. Since the tympanum is located deep in the ear canal, it is protected from tear or puncture. The eustachian tube drains excess fluid from the ear canal and regulates pressure, maintaining a healthy environment. The stapes is suspended by the stapedius muscle, which is triggered by levels of noise that will damage the cochlea. It limits the motion of the stapes and prevents it from transferring too much motion into the cochlea.

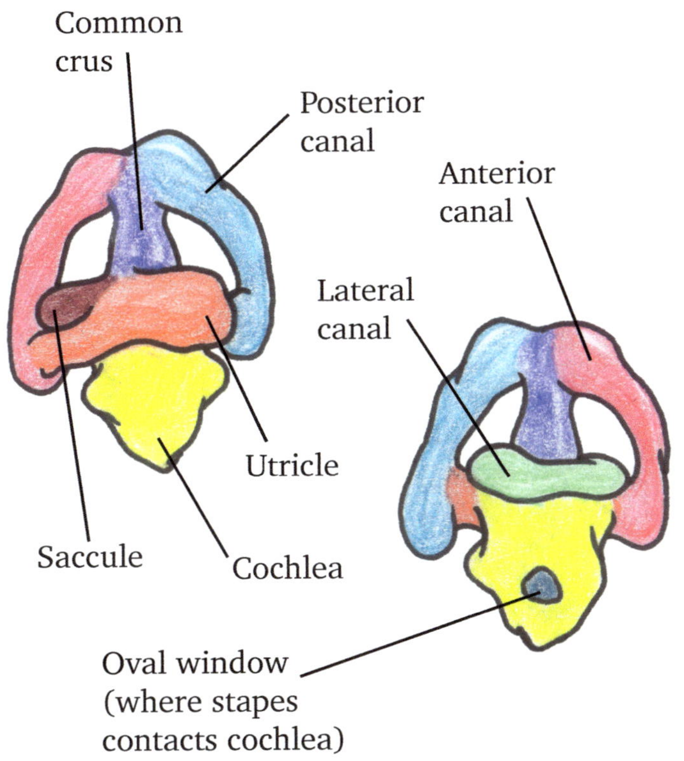

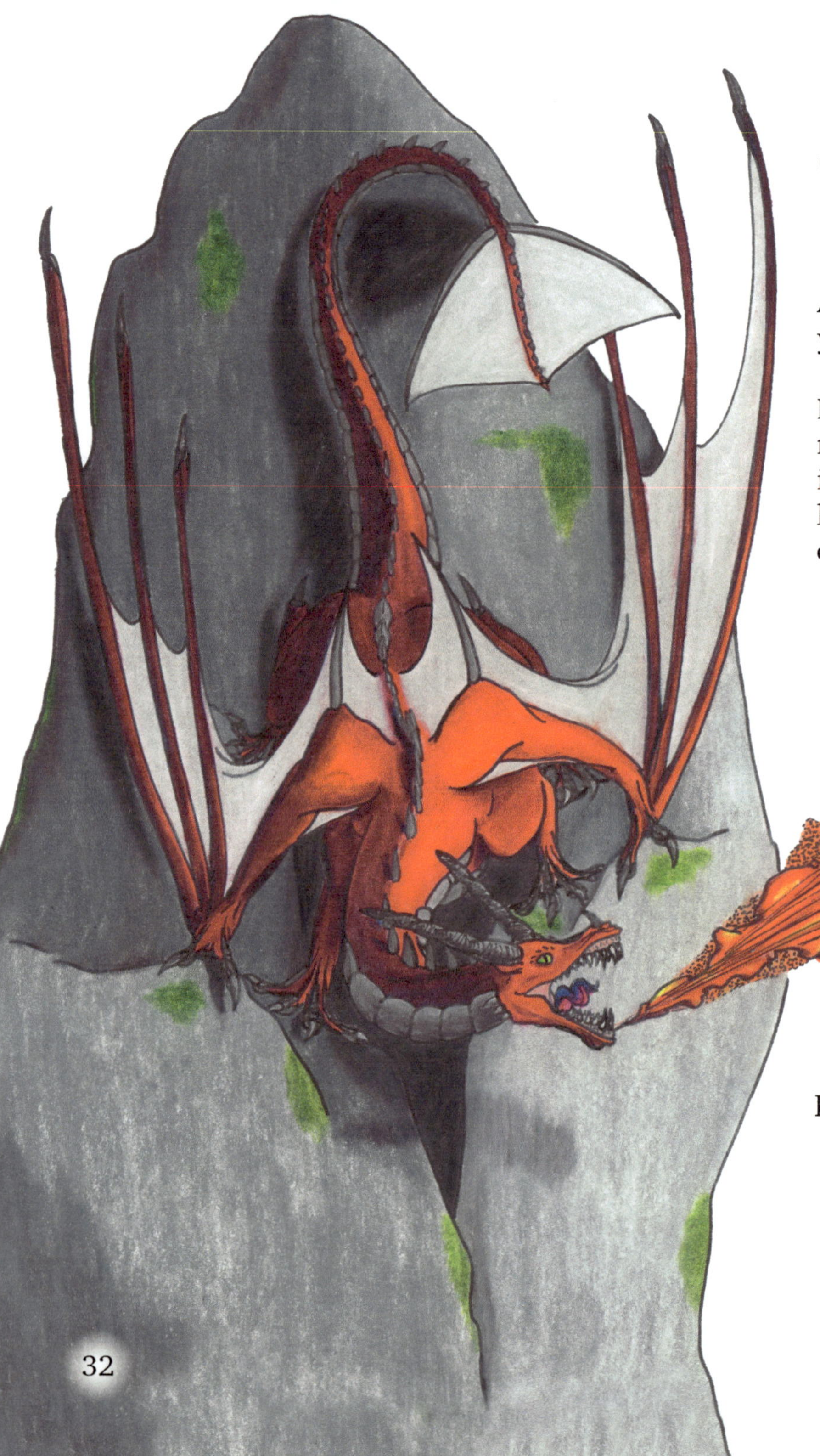

Closing

After reading this book, you might be having some doubts about your previous beliefs. That's normal.

However, this book was not made to snuff out your beliefs. It was made to spark new ones! If you are interested in anatomy, go for it. Draw, research, craft, create, imagine. If you have a question, look into it. The best question is one that leads to more particular questions and more plausible answers.

If this book did spark a new interest, look into careers related to biology. Biology is a big deal in today's world. Advances in medicine, the search for life in space and even the development of renewable fuels involve biology. Trailblazing biologists are all around us.

Never forget that the "impossible" is possible.

References

The Life Cycle (page 4):

Alligator Embryo. cdn.shopify.com/s/files/1/1731/3073/products/alligator-embryo_195x195@2x.jpg?v=1516652582.

WikiBooks. Female Bird Reproductive System. Digital image. WikiBooks. WikiBooks, n.d. Web. 29 Apr. 2016.

The Skin (page 6):

Desmarais, Anna. "'I Really Want to Touch It': U of A Experts Discover Dinosaur Skin Fossils." CBCnews, CBC/Radio Canada, 6 June 2017, 5:00 pm.

Klingenberg, Roger J., DVM. "Description and Physical Characteristics of Reptiles." The Merck Manual for Pet Health. The Merck Manual for Pet Health, July 2011. Web. 19 Mar. 2016.

Naish, Darren. "The Sensitive Face of a Big Predatory Dinosaur." Scientific American. Scientific American, 16 June 2017. Web. 20 Sept. 2018.

Salisbury, David. "Despite Their Thick Skins, Alligators and Crocodiles Are Surprisingly Touchy."

University of Bristol. "Characters and Anatomy." University of Bristol: Earth Sciences, University of Bristol, 2004.

The Foot (page 8):

WikipedianProlific. Morphology and Locomotive System of Equus Ferus Caballus (a Common Horse). Digital image. Wikipedia. Wikipedia, 29 July 2006. Web. 19 Mar. 2016.

The Wing (page 10):

Hagen, Elizabeth. "Human, Bird, and Bat Bone Comparison." ASU - Ask A Biologist. Arizona State University, 4 Nov. 2009. Web. 19 Mar. 2016.

Hutchinson, John R. "Vertebrate Flight: Pterosaurian Flight." Basic Flight Physics, UCMP Berkeley, 11 Jan. 1996.

LaBarbera, Katie. "Avian Flight I: Built for Flight." Tough Little Birds. Tough Little Birds, 22 Feb. 2013. Web. 19 Mar. 2016.

Myers, Phil. "Bat Wings and Tails." ADW: Animal Diversity Web. University of Michigan Museum of Zoology, 2016. Web. 19 Mar. 2016.

Pterosaurs to Birds. "Evolution of Feathers." Pterosaurs to Birds, Blogspot, Dec. 2016.

Science Learning. "Feathers and Flight." Science Learning Hub RSS. Science Learning, 16 Sept. 2011. Web. 19 Mar. 2016.

Speer, Brian R. "Chiroptera: More on Morphology." University of California Museum of Paleontology. University of California Museum of Paleontology, 20 Aug. 1995. Web. 19 Mar. 2016.

Than, Ker. "Why Bats Are More Efficient Flyers Than Birds." LiveScience. TechMedia Network, 22 Jan. 2007. Web. 25 Apr. 2016.

Witton, Mark. "Why the Giant Azhdarchid Arambourgiania Philadelphiae Needs a Fanclub." Mark Witton.com Blog, Mark Witton, 23 June 2016.

The Pouch (page 12):

Persons, W Scott, and Philip J Currie. The Tail of Tyrannosaurus: Reassessing the Size and Locomotive Importance of the M. Caudofemoralis in Non-Avian Theropods. The Anatomical Record, 2011, pp. 119–131, The Tail of Tyrannosaurus: Reassessing the Size and Locomotive Importance of the M. Caudofemoralis in Non-Avian Theropods.

The Egg (page 14):

Alligator Embryo. cdn.shopify.com/s/files/1/1731/3073/products/alligator-embryo_195x195@2x.jpg?v=1516652582.

Carr, Steven M. "Amniotic Egg." Memorial University, Memorial University, 2005.

Ehrlich, Paul R., David S. Dobkin, and Darryl Wheye. "Eggs and Their Evolution." Stanford University. Stanford University, 1988. Web. 29 Apr. 2016.

The Muscles (page 16):

Admin. Back Muscle Diagram Human Body. Digital image. Anatomy Human Body. Anatomy Human Body, 23 Mar. 2015. Web. 3 May 2016. <http://www.anatomy-diagram.info/anatomy-of-muscular-model-of-chest/back-muscle-diagram-human-body-3/>.

Encyclopædia Brittanica. Iliocostalis Muscle. Digital image. Encyclopædia Brittanica. Encyclopædia Brittanica, n.d. Web. 3 May 2016.

Merritt, Garrett. Lizard Pectoral Muscles. Digital image. SlidePlayer. SlidePlayer, 2011. Web. 25 Apr. 2016.

P., Jack. "Muscular System." Vet Blog. Google Blogs, 9 July 2012. Web. 2 May 2016.

Persons, W Scott, and Philip J Currie. The Tail of Tyrannosaurus: Reassessing the Size and Locomotive Importance of the M. Caudofemoralis in Non-

Avian Theropods. The Anatomical Record, 2011, pp. 119–131, The Tail of Tyrannosaurus: Reassessing the Size and Locomotive Importance of the M. Caudofemoralis in Non-Avian Theropods.

The Heart and Lungs (page 18):

Bird Air Sacs. d2r5da613aq50s.cloudfront.net/wp-content/uploads/369888.image0.jpg.

Campbell, Neil A. "Circulation and Gas Exchange." Campbell Biology, by Jane B. Reece et al., Pearson, 2011, pp. 897–903.

De Voe, Ryan S. "Reptilian Cardiovascular Anatomy and Physiology: Evaluation and Monitoring (Proceedings)." dvm360.Com, UBM, 1 Nov. 2010.

Encyclopædia Brittanica. "Different Animal Hearts." Encyclopædia Brittanica, Encyclopædia Brittanica, 2013.

Fernbank Science Center. "Respiration." Fernbank Science Center. Fernbank Science Center, n.d. Web. 19 Mar. 2016.

Geggel, Laura. "6 Strangest Hearts in the Animal Kingdom." LiveScience. TechMedia Network, 13 Feb. 2015. Web. 19 Mar. 2016.

LumenCandela. "Overview of the Circulatory System." LumenCandela, Open SUNY Textbooks.

Manisha, M. "Hearts of Different Vertebrates." BiologyDiscussion, BiologyDiscussion.

Ritchison, Gary. "Bird Respiratory System." Eastern Kentucky University. Eastern Kentucky University, n.d. Web. 19 Mar. 2016.

The Respiratory System. i.pinimg.com/originals/16/6a/f5/166af582e10682b4a8a949fdb251d834.jpg.

The Skeleton (page 20):

Admin. Human Skeletal System Diagram. Digital image. Anatomy Human Body. Anatomy Human Body, 24 Mar. 2015. Web. 3 May 2016. <http://www.anatomy-diagram.info/picture-of-blank-skelatal-system/human-skeletal-system-diagram/>.

Bestiarum Osteology. Frill-necked Lizard Skeleton (Chlamydosaurus Kingii). Digital image. Bestiarum Osteology. Bestiarum Osteology, n.d. Web. 25 Mar. 2016.

Carr, Thomas D., David J. Varrichio, Jayc C. Seldmayr, Eric M. Roberts, and Jason R. Moore. Tyrannosaurus Rex skull, labeled. Digital image. Scientific Reports. Nature.com, 30 Mar. 2017. Web. 19 Oct. 2018.

Comparison of Dinosaur Pelvises. Digital image. Miami University. Miami University, n.d. Web. 24 Apr. 2016.

Cryer, Brian. "Vertebral Column Explained." Everything Explained Today. Everything Explained Today, 2009-2016. Web. 25 Apr. 2016.

Dumont, Elizabeth R. "Bone Density and the Lightweight Skeletons of Birds." The Royal Society. The Royal Society, 17 Mar. 2010. Web. 19 Mar. 2016.

Fins to Feet. Triple Pelvis Comparison. Digital image. Fins to Feet. Fins to Feet, 14 July 2010. Web. 23 Apr. 2016.

Gandoza 3D Models. Giraffe Skeleton. Digital image. Gandoza 3D Models. Gandoza 3D Models, n.d. Web. 25 Apr. 2016.

Marshall Cavendish Corporation. "Elephant, Giraffe." Mammal Anatomy: An Illustrated Guide. Tarrytown, New York: Marshall Cavendish Corporation, 2010. 44-75. Google Books. Web. 19 Mar. 2016.

Savalli, Udo M. Labeled Bat Skeleton. Digital image. Udo M. Savalli, n.d. Web. 19 Mar. 2016.

The Skull and Brain (page 22):

Federation of American Societies for Experimental Biology (FASEB). "Scientists Find Surprise Lurking in Crocodilian Jaw." ScienceDaily. ScienceDaily, 04 Apr. 2016. Web. 19 Sept. 2018.

Geggel, Laura. "Giant Pterosaur Sported 110 Teeth (and 4 Wicked Fangs)." LiveScience. Purch, 13 Aug. 2018. Web. 21 Oct. 2018.

Gill. "Reptile Brain vs. Bird Brain." SlidePlayer, SlidePlayer.

Wikipedia. "Views of Sphenodon Skull." Wikiwand, Wikiwand.

WitmerLab: Alligator Brain, Nasal Cavity, and Other Air Spaces - Rolling Animation. Dir. WitmerLab. YouTube. WitmerLab, 07 Dec. 2008. Web. 20 Sept. 2018.

The Organs (page 24):

Durso, Andrew M. "Life Is Short, but Snakes Are Long." Why Do Snakes Have Two Penises? Google Blogger, 19 Mar. 2014. Web. 28 Apr. 2016.

Ehrlich, Paul R., David S. Dobkin, and Darryl Wheye. "Bird Voices." Stanford University. Stanford University, 1988. Web. 25 Apr. 2016.

Ehrlich, Paul R, et al. "Bird Milk." Stanford University, Stanford University, 1988.

Sasanami, T, et al. "Sperm Storage in the Female Reproductive Tract in Birds." PubMed.gov, NCBI, 2013.

WikiBooks. Female Bird Reproductive System. Digital image. WikiBooks. WikiBooks, n.d. Web. 29 Apr. 2016.

Wissman, Margaret A., D.V.M., D.A.B.V.P. "Reptiles: Reproduction "From Egg to Adult"" Exotic Pet Vet. Net. Exotic Pet Vet. Net, 2006. Web. 19 Mar. 2016.

Zug, George R. "Jacobson's Organ." Encyclopædia Britannica. Encyclopædia Britannica, 30 June 2014. Web. 28 Apr. 2016.

The Mouth (page 26):

Geggel, Laura. "Giant Pterosaur Sported 110 Teeth (and 4 Wicked Fangs)." LiveScience. Purch, 13 Aug. 2018. Web. 21 Oct. 2018.

The Eye (page 28):

Cow Eye Dissection, Labeled. anatomycorner.com/main/wp-content/images/eye-parts-removed-labeled.jpg.
The Cornell Lab Bird Academy. "All About Bird Anatomy." The Cornell Lab Bird Academy. The Cornell Lab of Ornithology, 2016. Web. 25 Apr. 2016.

Dubielzig, Dick. "Comparative Anatomy of the Vertebrate Eye & Evolution." University of Wisconsin-Madison, University of Wisconsin-Madison.

Insight Vision Center. "Human Vision Vs Eagle Vision." Insight Vision Center, Insight Vision Center, 8 July 2018.

Smithsonian Channel. "Astounding Facts About Crocodile Eyes." Smithsonian.com. Smithsonian Institution, n.d. Web. 18 Sept. 2018.

The Ear (page 30):

Bierman, Hilary S., and Catherine Emily Carr. "Sound Localization in the Alligator." PubMed.gov. U.S. National Library of Medicine, Nov. 2015. Web. 20 Oct. 2018.

Boistel, Renaud, Anthony Herrel, Gheylen Daghfous, Paul-Antoine Libourel, Elodie Boller, Paul Tafforeau, and Vincent Bels. "Assisted Walking in Malagasy Dwarf Chamaeleons." The Royal Society. The Royal Society, 12 May 2010. Web. 21 Oct. 2018.

Dufeau, David. Endosseous labyrinths of the left inner ear. Digital image. ResearchGate. ResearchGate, Jan. 2008. Web. 19 Oct. 2018.

Dufeau, David L., and Lawrence M. Witmer. "Ontogeny of the Middle-Ear Air-Sinus System in Alligator Mississippiensis (Archosauria: Crocodylia)." PLOS ONE. Public Library of Science, 23 Sept. 2015. Web. 20 Sept. 2018.

Eardoc. Inner Ear Diagram. Digital image. Eardoc. Eardoc, n.d. Web. 25 Apr. 2016.

Manley, Geoffrey. Representative examples of segmented endosseous labyrinths. Digital image. ResearchGate. ResearchGate, Feb. 2009. Web. 19 Oct. 2018.

About the Author

Dragons flew into Isabelle Busch's life in the first grade and never left. She is a scientist, artist, and nature enthusiast. Hiking by lakes, drawing on rainy afternoons and volunteering at local animal charities are her favorite activities. For the past 13 years, she has been a wildlife ambassador and fundraiser for CCF, the Cheetah Conservation Fund. She calls the state of Washington home.

Visit me at www.isabellebusch.com